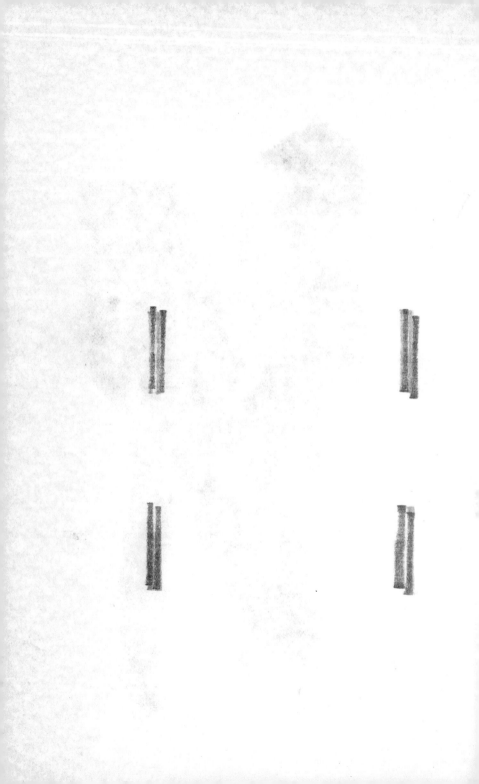

Gone to Glory

Moroni Traveler novels by Robert Irvine

The Angels' Share
Baptism for the Dead

other novels by the author

Ratings Are Murder
Footsteps
The Devil's Breath
Horizontal Hold
The Face Out Front
Freeze Frame
Jump Cut

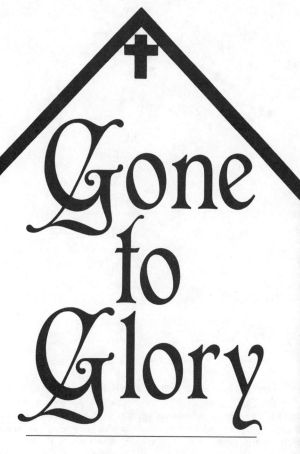

Gone to Glory

Robert Irvine

ST. MARTIN'S PRESS   NEW YORK

Library of Congress Cataloging-in-Publication Data
Irvine, R. R. (Robert R.)
        Gone to Glory / Robert Irvine.
                p.   cm.
        "A Thomas Dunne book."
        ISBN 0-312-04321-X
        I. Title.
    PS3559.R65G66   1990
    813'.54—dc20   89-78053

First Edition

10 9 8 7 6 5 4 3 2 1

To Albert and Angela Prata,
the greatest in-laws in the world

Gone to Glory

1

FOREIGN MONEY IS RUINING OUR TOWN.

The graffiti, three-foot letters sprayed in orange Day-Glo, ran along a temporary wall surrounding Salt Lake's latest construction site. The message dazzled Moroni Traveler's eyes but not his senses. He knew better than to believe everything he read, especially in a state like Utah. On occasion, he'd been called a foreigner himself for having once lived in California.

Traveler started the car and drove east on South Temple Street. Directly ahead stood the bronze statue of Brigham Young, one part of the landscape that would never change. He saluted the Mormon prophet and turned right, proceeding down Main Street. He had a 10 A.M. appointment with a boyhood idol by the name of Hap Kilgore. On the phone Kilgore had sounded old and weary, a far cry from Traveler's memory of him. But then Salt Lake wasn't what it used to be either.

On the left, a stone's throw from the statue, all that remained of the original Zion's Cooperative Mercantile Institution—ZCMI to the faithful—was a salvaged facade. Behind it stood an air-conditioned mall larger than the Mormon Choir's tabernacle.

A block farther on, there was no sign at all of the old

Studio Theatre, where Traveler and his teenage chum, Willis Tanner, had finally screwed up enough courage to buy tickets to their first French film, *Manon.*

The First National Bank Building had given way to First Security. But the name didn't change the way he felt about the place. There, on the fifth floor, Grandfather Ned Payson had practiced novocaine-free dentistry. Traveler's teeth clenched against the memory, against the old-fashioned drill, the crushing smell of ethyl chloride, and the clicking testament of Ned's own dentures.

To escape, Traveler peered into the rearview mirror. Brigham Young waved good-bye to him. It was a trick of light.

Traveler failed to make the traffic light at Second South and brought the Ford to a stop. On that corner, Second and Main, the sixteen-story Walker Bank Building had dominated the town since 1912, as had the Walker Brothers bankers in pioneer times. But while their building remained, the brothers' bastion of Gentile (non-Mormon) commerce had disappeared into the corporate shell of First Interstate. The old Owl Drug Store, a ground-floor tenant for decades, had surrendered its cigar counter and eternal flame to progress that went by the name Dean Witter.

Traveler rolled down the window. Exhaust fumes failed to hide the smell of a Utah spring: mountain sage, cottonwoods coming to leaf, the taste of promised rain in a morning sky that was still cloudless.

The light changed. Pulling out into the intersection he caught a glimpse of the Wasatch Mountains to the east. Each time he saw them they surprised him, snowcapped and deadly blue, a ten-thousand-foot reminder of winter no matter what the time of year in the valley below.

Eleven blocks to go, he thought. Brigham Young's blocks, seven to a mile. Part of the Mormon prophet's master plan, his town laid out according to holy logic, with all streets and avenues radiating out from its spiritual hub, the temple. Go south, as Traveler was doing, and the arteries progressed in numerical order. Go north and the same thing happened, as it did to the east and west. The only thing you had to remember was that the numbering system began at the temple itself, where adjacent streets had been baptized East Temple, North Temple, West Temple, and South Temple. Beyond them came First East, First North, First West, and First South. Farther out were the avenues and lettered streets, a rational progression all the way to the city limits. After that came the secular chaos of postwar growth. Greater Salt Lake it was called now, with over a million people and everything that went with them.

By Fifth South Traveler gave up looking for landmarks that no longer existed and switched on the radio. Normally it would have been pretuned to KBYU, the church station that played classical music. But his father had driven the Ford last, leaving behind one of those call-in talk shows.

"We have Howard on the line from Sugar House."

"I've got a joke I'd like to tell. It's about the pope in Rome, who gets a phone call from God."

"Remember where you are, Howard," the host said. "This is Mormon country, the land of Zion."

"It's not dirty."

"There's such a thing as sacrilege."

"Like I was saying, the pope gets this phone call from God."

"Would God have to use a phone, Howard?"

"Are you going to let me tell my story or not?"

"I'm listening."

"God calls the pope and says, 'I've got good and bad news. Which would you like first?' 'The good news, of course,' says the pope. 'All right,' God tells him, 'here's the deal. I've decided to end religious strife on earth by merging all churches into one, Jews, Christians, Muslims, everybody. No more bickering.' 'That's wonderful,' says the pope. 'But what's the bad news?' 'I'm calling from Salt Lake City,' God says.''

Traveler sought relief on KBYU, where the Mormon Tabernacle Choir kept his mind occupied until he reached Thirteenth South and turned right. Half a block ahead stood Derks Field, home of the Salt Lake City Saints baseball team. This time of the morning he had no trouble parking directly across the street from the concrete stadium.

As soon as he got out of the car, he heard lawn mowers in the outfield and smelled freshly cut grass. The scent carried memories of the old Pioneer League when Salt Lake's team had been called the Bees. It was the manager of those Bees, Hap Kilgore, who needed Traveler's kind of help.

The stadium's ticket windows were closed, but a gate on the left field side stood open. Traveler went in, half expecting to be challenged by some kind of security. Nobody paid any attention to him until a grounds keeper, riding a lawn-mowing tractor, waved him out of the way in order to maneuver the machine into a space under the bleachers. In his wake he left a perfectly manicured outfield where uniformed ball players were running windsprints and shagging fly balls.

Once the man switched off the engine and dismounted, he trotted over to Traveler and shook hands. "Hap Kilgore told me to keep an eye out for you. He's over there." He pointed across the diamond, just beyond first base where two men in uniform were hitting fungoes to the outfielders.

"I didn't realize he was still coaching," Traveler said.

The grounds keeper, who had the deeply lined face and neck of a man who worked in the sun, tugged at the bill of his Saints cap as if he were flashing signals to a base runner. "The old boy is a fixture around here. A kind of honorary coach, if you know what I mean."

Traveler kept quiet, hoping for elaboration.

"I used to watch you play when you were linebacking for L.A. You were something, you were." He shoved his cap back on his head and grinned. "Hap says you're a private detective now."

"That's right."

"I hope the old man's not in trouble."

Traveler answered with a noncommittal shrug.

"Come on. I'll let you into the grandstand. They don't like outsiders walking on the field, so you'll have to go around."

He pulled a wad of keys from a spring-loaded reel attached to his belt. One of them opened a green metal door set into the stadium's concrete base. He gave Traveler a gentle push. "There's another door on the right field side just like this one. It's never locked from the inside."

Underneath the grandstand the temperature was a good ten degrees cooler than outside. Sixty-five, Traveler guessed, compared with the seventy-five degrees of spring for which he'd dressed that morning. Blue denim workshirt, Levis, and what he still called tennis shoes, though Reebok had a more exotic name for them.

Whatever happened to Keds? he was wondering as he exited the grandstand a couple of minutes later. Halfway down the right field line the fungoe hitters were taking turns. While one hit, the other fielded throws from the outfielders with a catcher's mitt. From behind, their uniforms made them look interchangeable. Both wore the number 42. Both had the name Hoot Collins stitched across the shoulders.

A waist-high metal fence, fitted with a narrow gate, separated the playing field from foul ground where Traveler was now standing. He stepped to the chain-link and said, "I'm looking for Hap Kilgore."

Both men turned around. The one with the mitt had a chipmunk-cheek full of tobacco and a gut that sagged over his tightly cinched belt. He spit juice to clear his mouth. "Damn, it's good to see you again, Mo."

Traveler fought against surprise, tried to smile naturally. But his face felt tight and unyielding. All that remained of the Hap Kilgore he remembered, the boyhood icon, was his famous red-faced, blushing complexion. Everything else had weathered away.

"I'm taking a breather, Hooty," Kilgore told his companion.

Hooty, who carried the same weight but a lot fewer years, shrugged indifferently and went back to hitting fly balls with a metal bat.

Kilgore fired a shot of tobacco across Hooty's bow before opening the gate and moving in for a bear hug. Thirty years had gone by but Kilgore smelled the same, astringent enough to make Traveler's eyes water.

Relief pitcher's cologne, Hap had called it the first time they met. *Sloan's Liniment. Slap a little on your pitching arm and you're ready to go. No fuss, no muss.*

He ended the hug and stepped back to peer up at Traveler. "How the hell did you get so big? You must be a foot taller than your father."

"Not quite."

"I'll be goddamned just the same. I remember the first time he brought you to one of our games. You were big for your age, but not this big."

He took a pouch of Redman tobacco from his back pocket and reloaded his cheek. "No wonder you went into football."

"I didn't have any choice. I couldn't hit curves."

"Baseball's a bitch, isn't it? But I still love it. You know why?"

Traveler didn't answer, knew he wasn't expected to. Kilgore was talking to hide his nervousness, a common enough reaction when someone called in a private detective.

Even so, there was a little-boy glint in his eyes. "Where else could a man my age spit whenever he wants to and get away with it?"

He took off his cap to rub his bald head, a gesture of frustration that had been his trademark when he managed the old Bees. In those days his scalp had been as fiery red and shiny as the rest of him. Now it was spotted and wrinkled. His age, Traveler calculated, had to be somewhere in the sixties.

A ball got by Hooty and bounced against the fence. Kilgore spit at it and missed. "I'd better hit a few, Mo. Can you wait for a few minutes?"

"Of course."

"You're Martin's son, all right. You don't let a man down." With that, Kilgore went to get his bat. As soon as he started hitting fungoes the outfielders moved in fifty feet.

As a playing manager of the Bees, he'd been known to drive fielders all the way to the walls during batting practice. That wasn't easy at Derks, where it was 351 feet down the line in left, 365 in right, and well over 400 to the center field clubhouse.

But relief pitching, not hitting, had been his specialty, with a fastball that some said was a spitter. Whatever it was, he could strike out the best of them for an inning or two.

When Kilgore's fungoes ran out of steam, dribbling into grounders, he rejoined Traveler. "It's hell to get old." When he spit, tobacco trickled onto his shirt.

"You've lasted longer than I did in sports," Traveler said.

"I saw that article about you in the *Tribune*. You had bad luck. Simple as that. In baseball you can get beaned or spiked. In football, the odds of injury are higher, that's all. So you crippled a guy. He knew the chance he was taking. Still, I can understand how you felt. You came back home to start over as a detective. I came back to be with the Saints."

"And now you need my help?"

"I remember telling your dad once that you had the look of someone who'd follow in his father's footsteps. But that was a long time ago, something I'd forgotten about until I saw Moroni Traveler and Son listed in the phone book."

His hand went to his bald head. His fingers moved slowly, as if searching for hair. "The first time I met Martin was in a bar, the Zang."

Kilgore spit again, this time with more precision. "I went looking for the place the other day but couldn't find it."

"It's a rib joint now."

"I used to hang out there with a couple of my older players. They weren't going anywhere, so they didn't need a curfew. We'd arm wrestle for beers. Your dad took all three of us the first time we met him. How tall is he, for God's sake? Five-six?"

"Thereabouts."

"He's not a man to be taken at face value, that's for sure."

"He played tennis at the university, you know."

"I do now. His right arm is twice as big as his left, for Christ's sake. I never did see that man pay for a beer, not when there was someone to arm wrestle."

"Martin seldom drinks these days."

"That's another thing. If his name is Martin and yours is Moroni, how come the business is called *Moroni Traveler and Son?*"

"Ever since he was a kid, Dad insisted on calling himself Martin. He hates being named for an angel."

"I can't say I blame him."

Growing up, Traveler had been tempted to call himself Martin, too. But his mother wouldn't hear of it. *You're*

*named for the Angel Moroni, she'd drummed into him.
Every time I see the temple I say to myself, "My son's
namesake is up there. His golden likeness is blowing a
trumpet to call the faithful to Zion."*

"When you called, you said you needed help," Traveler
reminded him. "You said your life needed saving."

Kilgore caught Hooty's eye. Hooty nodded and said,
"Don't worry about me. I'm doing fine."

Kilgore took hold of Traveler's arm and led him down
the right field line toward the bull pen. When they reached
the pitching rubber, Kilgore perched on it. "Jesus, this
brings back memories." He squinted as if to keep the light
of day from leaking into his past. "They got rid of the Bees
when they tried to push Salt Lake into the Pacific Coast
League. When that flopped this town didn't have a team
until the Saints started up. But the Saints aren't my Bees,
not by a long shot."

Traveler agreed but kept it to himself. Saying so would
keep Kilgore from coming to the point.

The old man went through his pitching motion. "I
never made it to the big leagues, either as a player or a
manager. But I've been all over this country. In Dodger
Stadium, Yankee Stadium, and a lot of stadiums in between. And you know something? This is still my favorite
ballpark. Look at that view, for Christ's sake."

He pointed toward the Wasatch Mountains. "There's
inspiration for you. Ten thousand feet of rock and ice that
Brigham Young crossed to get here. One hell of a lot of
faith went into that."

Traveler concentrated on the left field bleachers instead
of the mountains. A man was sitting in the front row, ap-
parently watching them through binoculars.

"I'm here on faith, too," he said after a moment.

"You're young. You're in a hurry. But I'm coming to
the point. Do you remember Pepper Dalton?"

"I was here the day Pepper hit his one and only home run."

Tickets to that game had been a birthday present from his father, along with a picnic dinner and all the hot dogs, popcorn and soda that he and his best friend, Willis Tanner, could eat.

"No-hit Dalton we called him," Kilgore said. "But he was the greatest fielding shortstop I ever coached, with an arm like a Springfield rifle. And fast on his feet. Shit, he was a threat to steal every time he got on base. Of course, that was the problem. If you don't hit, you don't get to first base, do you?"

He sighed. "You've got to remember, the Bees were C League. If you don't hit at that level, and I mean *hit*, you don't move up in the farm system. Sometimes, if you're really good with the glove, they give you a couple of years to come around. But if you don't produce then, you're out on your ass. I stuck out my neck for Pepper. I gave him three seasons with the Bees. You know what he hit on his best year?"

Traveler knew all right. After that birthday home run, Pepper Dalton had supplanted Hap as his hero. Thinking back now, it was the only birthday gift he could remember from childhood.

"I'll tell you," Kilgore went on. "One-sixty-one, and that was after two years of me working with him. I cashed in favors to bring in a batting instructor from the Coast League. Hopeless, the guy told me. Turn him into a pitcher. I tried. But curveballs hurt Pepper's arm. Even so, I stuck with him. It cost me a promotion. Why—"

"Hey, Hap," Hooty called. "Jo-Jo's arrived. You'd better start hitting a few."

"Jo-Jo's the manager," Kilgore explained. "Come on. I can talk and hit at the same time."

"And Hooty?"

"Aw, what the hell. He can hear the rest of what I have to say."

But Hooty didn't stick around to eavesdrop. Instead, he hustled into the dugout as soon as Hap took up the bat. The outfielders moved in again. Hap spit tobacco juice on a ball, then whacked it over their heads.

"That'll teach those young bucks a little respect. Toss me another ball."

Traveler obliged.

"Watch this."

Kilgore swung too hard and popped it up. A fielder broke in at a dead run, caught it one-handed, and threw it back as if he were trying to nail someone at home plate.

Traveler stepped in front of the old man and knocked the ball down bare-handed.

"Better put on the mitt, Mo. Otherwise you might get hurt."

Traveler looked around. No one seemed to be paying any attention, so he did as requested.

Kilgore picked up another ball and hit a medium fly. "The truth is, I liked Pepper's style. We're still close after all these years, you know. Very close."

Traveler fielded the throw in and lobbed the ball to Kilgore. The old man rubbed it for a moment before tossing it in the air. He swung hard, grunting with the effort, and missed.

"Took my eye off it, for Christ's sake." Breath wheezed out of him along with tobacco juice. "Pepper used to do the same damned thing."

"Let me try hitting a few," Traveler said, rolling up his sleeves.

"Why not. You look like you've kept yourself in good enough shape."

The metal bat felt strange in Traveler's hands, much lighter than the wooden ones he remembered from American Legion ball. His first toss of the ball was so far off-center that he didn't swing. When he glanced at the outfielders he could see them edging in.

Kilgore snorted and spit. "They're making a mistake with a man your size."

Traveler swung easily. The ball went about three hundred feet, more than the fielders had expected but still catchable. His next one, a line drive, sent them back to the base of the left field wall.

"That's where Pepper hit his homer," Kilgore said.

Traveler squinted toward the metal fence where billboards advertised Mullet-Kelly Men's Clothes, the I & M Rug and Linoleum Company, the Mayflower Café, and Pay Less Drug Stores. He'd hit the fence once as a seventeen-year-old American Legion All-Star. Since then he'd grown half a foot and fifty pounds.

"Don't try to kill it," Kilgore advised as if he could read Traveler's mind. "Uppercut it a bit. You'll be surprised what these metal bats can do. It's a good thing they don't use them in pro ball, otherwise no pitcher would be safe."

At the crack of the bat Traveler knew he'd connected squarely. So did the outfielders. Instead of giving chase they merely turned to watch the ball clear one of the light standards.

"Jesus H. Christ," Kilgore said. "If Pepper had only been able to hit like that." He spit. "One home run in three years. No wonder nobody but us remembers him."

Traveler took a deep breath, savoring the smell of Sloan's Liniment and new-mown grass. For a moment, just as he hit another ball out of the park, he thought he could smell hot dogs, too, and roasted peanuts.

"Ease off," Kilgore said. "Balls cost money."

Traveler stretched, enjoying the feel of the hot sun on his shoulders. Kilgore tossed him another ball.

When Traveler caught it, he felt like a kid again.

Twelve years old, with the Bees playing their archrival, the New York Yankee farm team from Twin Falls, Idaho. His father had given him birthday tickets so that the three of them, Willis Tanner included, could go to the game.

They had arrived at Derks Field two hours early to get their favorite seats, the last row up in the grandstand directly in front of the radio booth. From there they could watch the game and hear the announcer call the play-by-play at the same time.

Traveler adjusted his swing. The outfielders, who'd been bunched along the warning track, vied to see who would catch it. Two of them collided. The ball dropped free.

"Call for it," Kilgore muttered, though not loud enough for anyone but Traveler to hear it. "That could cost you a game."

By the time the Bees game started, mustard stains were all that remained of his and Willis's hot dogs. Ice cream and soda pop had left their fingers sticky. Peanut shells crunched underfoot each time they stomped encouragement for the Bees.

Traveler found his rhythm, sending fly ball after fly ball to the base of the wall. He was hitting the balls faster than Kilgore could feed them to him.

Not a run scored until the top of the ninth, when an error gave Twin Falls the lead, one to nothing. In the radio booth behind them, the announcer lamented, "I hate to say it, folks, but the Bees have the weak end of their order due up in their half of the inning, the six, seven, and eight hitters."

Traveler paused to wipe sweat from his eyes.

"Give me the bat," Hap said. "I'll spell you."

The outfielders booed.

The booing started when the Bees number-six hitter struck out. While number seven, Ed Tomkins, was on his way to the plate, the booth announcer said, "There's sure to be a pinch hitter for Pepper Dalton, who's due up next. Only trouble is, Hap Kilgore has already used up most of his bench. But he's still got Matt Hensen, the backup catcher, or even one of his better-hitting pitchers."

The crowd buzzed.

"Call me a liar," said the announcer. "We've got a pinch hitter right now. Hensen is out of the dugout and swinging a bat. He's going to hit for Tomkins."

The Twin Falls manager came out onto the field to talk to his left-hander on the mound. From there, the two of them stared intently at Pepper Dalton, who was now warming up in the on-deck circle.

When pitcher and manager nodded at each other, the crowd grew silent.

"They're walking Hensen intentionally," the announcer confirmed a moment later.

Traveler was about to swing the metal bat again when Kilgore laid a restraining hand on his shoulder. "That's enough, son. You're making the rest of us look bad."

Traveler smiled at the old man but was still seeing him as he once was.

Kilgore stepped out of the dugout, removed his hat with one hand and rubbed his bald head with the other, then walked slowly over to the on-deck circle. He didn't say anything to Dalton, but only clapped him on the back and shoved him toward the plate, surprising everyone, including the announcer.

"I don't like to second-guess, folks, but all I can say is that Pepper's hitting one-fifty-nine. Wait a minute. Twin Falls is bringing in another pitcher. A sidearming right-hander. That has to be it for Pepper Dalton."

Pepper acted as if he'd heard the announcer himself. He took an uncertain step toward the dugout, but Kilgore waved him back toward the plate. Fans began heading for the exits to beat traffic rather than wait for the inevitable.

Dalton bailed out on the first pitch, a fastball on the inside corner.

Traveler crossed his fingers and showed them to Willis, who did the same.

"You gotta know the curve's coming next," the announcer said. *His tone of voice said that would be the end of Dalton.*

The next pitch looked to be inside. Dalton's front foot twitched out of the way as the curveball broke sharply. His foot was still on the move as he swung in desperation.

The crowd was so stunned that the broadcaster's voice echoed in the grandstand. "That ball's really hit. It's going . . . going . . . it's gone to glory."

"Whew." Kilgore took a red-checkered bandana from his back pocket and mopped sweat from his face. "What do you say, Mo? I think we've earned ourselves a breather."

Traveler suddenly noticed how pale the old man had become.

"Let's get you out of the sun," he said.

Kilgore shook his head and gestured toward the dugout, where two middle-aged men in uniform were talking. "That's a management huddle going on in there. It's safer out here."

He tied the bandana around his head like a sweatband. "Besides, you know what they say about fresh air—it's good for us old farts."

"Come on, Hap," came a shout from the outfield. "We're waiting out here."

Grimacing, Kilgore thrust his arms into the air in a signal of surrender. The outfielders answered with obscene gestures before forming into pairs to run windsprints along the base of the outfield fence.

"You see that? Young players these days have no respect."

"Did you at their age?"

Kilgore chuckled. "I guess not." He took the metal bat from Traveler and leaned on it. Despite the improvised sweatband, runoff was still dripping into his eyes.

For his part, Traveler felt chilled. He rolled down his

shirtsleeves and buttoned the cuffs. "You've got to be careful this time of year. The sun feels hot, but the air is still cool."

"A man my age has to be careful, you mean." Kilgore made a face as he squinted toward the Wasatch Mountains, where thunderheads were beginning to boil around the edges of the snow-covered peaks. "There's nothing like Mormon country in May. The weather can change just like that." He snapped his fingers. "Sun one minute, rain the next."

The breeze blowing off the mountains carried with it the promise of rain. Thunder rumbled in the distance.

"Jesus," Kilgore said, tossing the bat toward the dugout. "Here I am standing around with a lightning rod in my hand." He pointed his nose at the outfielders. "Wouldn't that give those young bucks a laugh, me getting zapped?"

"That's a metal fence they're running along," Traveler pointed out.

Kilgore shifted tobacco from one cheek to the other before spitting toward left field. "You're right. It would serve them right if they got their asses singed."

He glanced over his shoulder in the general direction of the dugout. "Sometimes I think nobody around here has any brains. I mean, look at those guys. There are metal railings everywhere. Jo-Jo's leaning against one right now, for God's sake."

"The storm's still a long way off," Traveler said.

"Dummies, every one," Kilgore went on, undeterred. "But that's one thing you can't say about Pepper Dalton. He was no dope. The fact is, he was the smartest player I ever coached. That home run of his, for instance. He knew right off that it was the highlight of his career. 'Quit while you're ahead,' I told him. And you know what he said? 'You're right, Hap. I'm not good enough. I never will be.'"

The old man stared toward the mountains and sighed. His eyes had the long look of someone focusing on the past. "Pepper wasn't your average player, not by a long shot. Most of these boys fool themselves. Next season's always going to be their big year, the one that will put them in the major leagues. But not Pepper. He never lied to himself. You know what he said to me after that game? 'Hap,' he said, 'I'm hanging 'em up at the end of this season. But I'll be back one day, running things my way.'"

The old man stared Traveler in the face, waiting to be prompted.

"What did he mean by that?" Traveler supplied.

"He became a student of the game. Spent twenty years managing in the minor leagues just like me, getting himself ready to own his own team. There's only one problem with that, of course. Managing in the minors pays spit. Pepper couldn't save any more than I could."

Traveler raised his hands, palms up, a silent question about the relevance of what the old man was saying.

"Hold your horses. I'm coming to the point."

Traveler dropped his hands far enough to slide them into the pockets of his Levis.

"Lady luck stepped in. Pepper inherited money. Last week he made an offer for the Saints, and it was accepted."

Kilgore wet his lips, his tongue policing up shreds of tobacco. When he opened his mouth to say something more, he hiccupped. The spasm caused him to swallow his mouthful of Redman. His Adam's apple shimmied. He doubled over, gagging and spitting repeatedly to rid himself of what shreds remained in his mouth.

When he raised his head a few moments later there were tears in his eyes. "I was going to be his third base coach."

"Was?"

"Pepper was arrested this morning."

Before Traveler could react a voice called from the dugout. "Hey, Hap. Have you got a minute?"

"I'd better see what Jo-Jo wants."

"Why was he arrested?"

Kilgore shook his head and started for the dugout, reloading his mouth with tobacco. Halfway there he stopped and turned around. "They say he killed his own sister to get the money."

2

WHILE HAP SPOKE WITH the Saints' manager, Traveler lounged against the metal fence and kept his eyes on the gathering thunderheads. The rain smell was stronger than ever, but so far the clouds showed no signs of making it over the mountains. But then the Wasatch had a tradition of keeping things out. They'd served as Brigham Young's barrier against his enemies in the east. Against Missouri Pukes, as Mormons called them, and the Illinois Satanists who'd persecuted the faithful from the beginning, stealing their land and murdering their first prophet, Joseph Smith. Once those mountains had held up a federal army long enough to keep Brigham Young from being arrested for treason.

Traveler lowered his eyes. The man in the left field bleachers was still there watching through binoculars.

Traveler leaned back, stretching. Directly overhead, the brilliant spring sky, still untouched by eastern thunderheads, was split down the middle by the contrail of a jet passing over the mountains. It made him wonder how Brigham would cope these days against the forces of change.

Moving slowly, nonchalantly, he ambled back toward the grandstand. Once hidden from bleacher view by the concrete structure, he broke into a trot, bypassing the metal doors to circle the stadium.

He reached the bleachers without being seen. The snooper, dressed in nondescript gray, hadn't moved.

Traveler got within a few feet before the man sensed his presence and jerked the binoculars away from his face. His bloodshot eyes widened with fear. He tried to back up but the bleacher seats had him trapped.

"I got permission," he blustered.

"To do what?"

"Scout around, by golly."

Traveler moved in so close the man sat down abruptly on the wooden slat beneath him.

"Big guys like you don't scare me." His pinched face said otherwise.

At best he was half Traveler's two hundred and twenty pounds.

"Who are you?" Traveler said.

"Golly. Golly Simpson."

Traveler held out his hand, palm up, demanding proof. Gingerly, the man took out his wallet and extracted a card.

Traveler shook his head.

"You got no right," he said, but handed over his wallet anyway.

The name on the driver's license was Gulliver Simpson. His calling card read GULLIVER "GOLLY" SIMPSON. Beneath the name was the word INVESTMENTS.

"Who are you watching?" Traveler said. "Me or Kilgore?"

"I'm a scout for the Butte team."

"Montana is a long way from here."

"I'm free-lance."

"If I see you again," Traveler said, "I'll know you're lying."

3

TRAVELER WAS BACK IN right field, leaning against the fence with his eyes closed, when Kilgore shouted in his ear.

"The fuckers have let me go. Fired me. Told me to get lost."

The old man clenched trembling fists in Traveler's face. One of them held a dilapidated gym bag, which Kilgore began waving like a weapon.

Traveler stepped back, out of range, while a thought nagged at him. Had his unauthorized presence on the field been to blame? "What happened?"

The gym bag sagged against Kilgore's hip. "There's only one reason I can think of. With Pepper in jail, the deal's fallen through. As of now, they don't think I have any . . ." He pulled at his lower lip as if feeling for a word that eluded him.

"Clout," Traveler supplied.

"Exactly. The sons-a-bitches think I'm just some old man they can kick around."

The flush had left his face. Without color, his skin was as lifeless as undertakers' art. His uniform, which had looked skintight around the belly only moments ago, now seemed baggy. The bulge of tobacco in his cheek seemed ominous, like a tumor.

In frustration, he drop-kicked the gym bag. It landed near the dugout. "Those assholes can't fire me. I'm a volunteer."

In one quick motion Kilgore pulled the uniform top over his head. Underneath he wore a dark blue turtleneck sweatshirt. Once uncovered, the garment radiated Sloan's Liniment strong enough to repel bugs.

"The shirt's theirs. So are the pants."

With that, he undid his belt and zipper and collapsed onto the grass to remove the rest of his uniform. His rubber-cleated baseball shoes came first, followed by his pants. Finally he rolled down his blue knee-high baseball socks to reveal white, hairless legs that looked too thin to support the rest of him. He made no move to jettison his sweat socks.

"You know what they pay me, Mo?" Kilgore struggled onto his knees before lurching to his feet. "A free fucking pass to the games if the stands aren't full. On a big night, I have to watch from the bull pen. By God, when we get Pepper out of jail things are going to be different around here. A third base coach, even in this league, is nothing to be sneezed at."

"Don't expect miracles," Traveler said. "I'm not a bail bondsman."

"Even an old fart like me knows you can't make bail for murder. That means you're going to have to prove that Pepper is innocent."

"That's what lawyers are for."

"A lawyer's fine, but *you* I know."

"Get dressed and we'll go somewhere else to talk."

Kilgore waved away the suggestion. "They're not running me out of here like some kid who's snuck in over the fence. I'm taking my own good time about it."

He walked over to his gym bag, unzipped it and removed a pair of tightly rolled, gray work trousers. Once unfurled, they were as wrinkled as old newspaper. He gave them a perfunctory jerk to smooth them out, then balanced precariously on one foot and tried to pull them over the other.

Traveler caught him as he was about to fall. Laughter spilled out of the dugout.

Kilgore spit disgustedly. "You saw me play, Mo. I used to be like a cat when I got out on that pitcher's mound."

"Come on. Use me as a prop. That way we'll get out of here faster."

The old man clenched his teeth. The rest of him shook in frustration but he held on to Traveler just the same. When his trousers were finally in place, he slipped his feet into tennis shoes that looked old enough to be Keds. The last item out of the gym bag was a bright orange down-filled vest, the kind hunters wear. From one of its pockets he produced a small can of spray deodorant, which he turned on himself to kill the smell of liniment.

"I'm ready," he said, handing the gym bag to Traveler.

The moment Kilgore's hands were free, he scooped up his uniform and wadded it into a bundle the size of a medicine ball. Then he grinned at Traveler. "I won't be needing a Saints rig anymore. Pepper's going to change the name back to the Bees."

With that, he spit tobacco juice onto the uniform and hurled it into the dugout, missing Jo-Jo by less than a foot.

Kilgore laughed so hard he hiccupped. That caused him to swallow again. He tried to spit but the tobacco was already on its way to his stomach. Even so, he managed an obscene gesture at the dugout.

As soon as the manager started up the concrete steps, Traveler grabbed Kilgore by the elbow and hustled him through the gate and under the grandstand. There, the fight drained out of the old man. He sagged against Traveler and made a gagging sound. After a moment he wheezed, "A man my age ought to know better than to chew tobacco."

"What you need is a drink."

"Coffee, if it's all the same to you."

"Where would you like to go?"

"The old Bees hangout, Fred and Kelly's on State Street."

4

FRED AND KELLY'S was a relic from the past, a drive-in on the outside and a café with booths and a counter inside. The architecture was that streamlined stucco from the 1930s with rounded edges and porthole windows. Because it was late for breakfast and early for lunch, they had the place to themselves.

"I'm buying," Kilgore announced with enthusiasm that sounded forced.

"I'll include it in my expenses," Traveler said. He'd already assumed that his usual fees were beyond the old man's capabilities. Whether or not he'd ever see money from Pepper Dalton was moot at this point.

The waitress was a relic of the present. Her earphones were wired into a portable cassette player clipped to her belt. Whatever she was listening to had erased all sign of animation from her face.

"What will it be?" she said, her mouth moving carefully, as if she were lip-syncing someone else's words.

"Two coffees," Traveler told her.

As an afterthought, he held up two fingers to make certain that he'd gotten through.

Once they'd been served Traveler went to work. "All right, Hap. You'd better tell me everything."

The old man's hands crawled across the table to wrap themselves around his coffee mug. "If Pepper has to stay in jail, his dream will die. Both of us will be out of baseball for good."

"Stick to the killing."

"You're right. I'm rambling like a senile old man."

Kilgore poured enough sugar into his coffee to shock a diabetic. "It began about ten years ago. Pepper and his sister, Priscilla—Prissy, everybody called her, and with good reason—inherited an abandoned coal mine and the town that went with it. Their grandfather had bought the place sometime after the war. By then, of course, there were better pickings to be had elsewhere. Oil was kicking the crap out of coal prices. Things like that. It's no wonder the place became a ghost town. Shit. We're talking the Pavant Mountains near the old state capital of Fillmore. Glory, it's called. Glory, Utah. Population, God only knows."

Kilgore paused to test his coffee. He made a face and added cream. "These days Glory is full of religious squatters. Polygamists chasing everything in skirts, Prissy Dalton included."

Only in Utah, Traveler thought. Where Joseph Smith's revelation from God gives no slack, either to the faithful or to those who merely seek justification for their lust. *For behold, I reveal unto you a new and an everlasting covenant; and if ye abide not that covenant, then are you damned.*

"My father has a cardinal rule," Traveler said. "Never stick your nose in church business."

"I'm not talking the LDS Church here," Kilgore said. "These fruitcakes call themselves the Flock, or some such nonsense."

"When it comes to religion in this state, the Mormon Church is always involved."

The old man fingered the tip of his sun-ruined nose. "It never occurred to me that you might be LDS."

"I'm not," Traveler said.

"Like father, like son, eh? The Word of Wisdom never cut no ice with Martin, that's for sure. Not the way he used to down those beers at the Zang."

The Word of Wisdom was another of Joe Smith's pronouncements, known as WOW among the faithful. No tobacco, no liquor, no coffee, no tea, no artificial stimulants.

"Like I was saying, Mo, Prissy's been living down there ever since the inheritance. Screwing her polygamous head off for all I know, though I don't like speaking ill of the dead."

"And Pepper?"

"After he lost his last managing job in baseball, Triple-A it was too, he settled in Fillmore. That way he could be close to Prissy without having to live out to hell-and-gone in those mountains. At least Fillmore has a sandlot team. They were glad to get him, too."

Kilgore finished his coffee and pointed at Traveler's cup. "Are you drinking that?"

"Help yourself."

Winking, Kilgore exchanged cups. "Yes, sir. If you

hadn't told me better, I'd think you were a real LDSer. Sitting here, letting a good cup of coffee go to waste. No sign of cigarettes either. Hell, I haven't even heard you swear. That always makes me suspicious in Utah. I saw an article in the paper the other day. It said there are counties in this state where ninety percent of the people are Latter-day Saints."

He took his cap from the bench seat beside him and covered his bald head, adjusting the brim to eye level. "If you ask me, they're all a bunch of closet polygamists. But aren't we all when we're young? Christ, when I was your age, I'd screw anything in skirts."

He stared out the window as if his past would be there if only he looked hard enough. What was there, Traveler saw, was Golly Simpson in a tan Chevy four-door. The man grinned at them and waved.

"When you come right down to it," Kilgore went on, "wisdom is nothing more than a lack of testosterone."

Traveler nodded toward the parking lot. "Do you know the guy in the tan car?"

Kilgore squinted. "Should I?"

"He was at the ballpark."

Kilgore shook his head. "I haven't got my glasses with me, Mo."

Traveler eased out of the booth. "Could be it's me he's watching."

Smoke belched from the Chevy's exhaust pipe. As soon as Traveler took a step toward the door, the car raced from the parking lot.

"That's the trouble with having a past," Traveler said when he sat down again, staring the old man in the eye. "It can catch up with you at the wrong time."

Kilgore reached out hesitantly, his fingers stopping short of contact with Traveler's hand. He spoke quickly, as if to hide any thought of intimacy. "Where were we?"

"We were talking about Glory," Traveler said.

The old man sighed. His hand retreated. "That's right. I said 'Glory hallelujah' when Pepper and Prissy got an offer for the mine. Hell, it was for the whole damned town—lock, stock and barrel. Enough money so that Pepper could buy a baseball team with his half of the proceeds. But Prissy wouldn't have it. She said the people living there in Glory would have no place to go if she sold out. Even when Pepper told her she could buy them someplace better, she wouldn't listen. God had brought them to Glory, she said, and that was where they'd stay."

The coffee mug trembled in Kilgore's hand. "Do you know what Pepper said to that?"

Traveler shook his head as was expected of him.

"That she was hypnotized. That Zeke Eldredge had her under his spell."

The name rang a bell, and Kilgore noticed Traveler's reaction.

"You've heard of him, huh?"

The Eldredge that Traveler had in mind was a self-proclaimed preacher who claimed to speak for God. He nodded.

Kilgore wet his lips. His tongue found a shred of soggy tobacco, which he scraped into his mouth with his teeth.

"How big is the inheritance?" Traveler asked.

"Pepper never did tell me exactly. But it was enough to buy the Saints, so I guess he was going to be a millionaire."

"Who's buying the mine?"

"*That* he did tell me. The Deseret Coal and Gas Company."

"Shit," Traveler muttered. The word *Deseret* came from *The Book of Mormon.* It stood for honey bee. The beehive was Utah's state symbol. "It sounds like church money to me."

Kilgore dug into his pocket. Out came a pouch of Redman. Using two fingers he dipped a pinch and slipped it into his cheek.

"I like the way you think, Mo. The church buying in." He smacked his lips. "That would be one way of getting rid of polygamists, wouldn't it? But me and Pepper don't care who the money comes from. We just want to buy the Saints and turn them back into the Bees."

"What kind of relationship did he have with his sister?"

"They were close in the old days, before Prissy took up with Eldredge. Of course, she was always a little strange. All you've got to do is see Glory for yourself and you'll know what I mean. A woman would have to be crazy to want to live in that place when she could sell it and move to a mansion in Salt Lake."

"What you've told me so far gives Pepper a good motive for murder."

"Not if you knew him the way I do. Besides, just last week things were back to normal between them. She had a change of heart and was coming up to the city to sign the papers. But when she got here, Prissy was still the same old Prissy. Took one look around and said Salt Lake was the new Sodom and Gomorrah, which was Zeke Eldredge talking if I ever heard it. Anyway, she and Pepper got into one hell of an argument in the lobby of their hotel, the old Semloh down on South State. There must have been a dozen witnesses. Which is probably why they arrested him this morning when they found her body right in his room. I mean, for God's sake. Would a killer leave a body in his own room? Anyway, we were having a team meeting, just the two of us, when they nabbed him. I tried to vouch for him but they wouldn't listen."

The more Kilgore said the worse it sounded for Dalton. "Did Pepper have anything to say for himself?"

"You gotta understand. There wasn't much time. The police came storming into the dining room where we were eating breakfast. 'Are you Rick Dalton?' they asked. As soon as he said, 'That's me,' they handcuffed him and took him out. All he had time to say to me was, 'Find me some help, Hap.' I've been running around like a chicken with its head off ever since. It wasn't until an hour ago that I remembered you and your father."

Kilgore slid toward the aisle and looked up and down the café as if searching for a spittoon. "She was killed with a Louisville Slugger. I saw the police taking it away myself, wrapped in plastic. I know my baseball bats, Mo. That was a heavy, thirty-six-inch model. Pepper always used a light bat, no more than thirty-three inches long."

Traveler couldn't help smiling. He expected the same from the old man. But all Kilgore did was pluck a couple of paper napkins from a dispenser and wipe his mouth, surreptitiously relieving the buildup of tobacco.

"I heard them talking in the lobby later," he went on. "Someone said they saw a woman going into Pepper's room. They think it was his sister. I say it had to be the woman he was going to marry, Kate Ferguson."

"Did you tell the police that?"

"Sure, but when they went looking for Kate they couldn't find hide nor hair of her, not that they tried all that hard. I can't blame them much. I must have looked like some kind of lunatic, standing there in the hotel wearing the shirt half of my old Bees uniform. I only did it to celebrate the deal. Of course, that was before Prissy turned on us."

"Someone must have seen Pepper's lady friend." Traveler could hear the skepticism in his voice. "The desk clerk, for instance."

"Pepper and Kate were staying together all right. But you'd have to know Kate to understand why she wouldn't sign the register as Mrs. Dalton. That's not her style, not until after the wedding. The room was in Pepper's name only."

Kilgore pulled another wad of napkins from the tabletop

dispenser and absently wiped his mouth. "Right after the cops left with him, I saw that bastard Eldredge. Right there in the lobby, which was goddamned strange since Prissy said once that he'd taken an oath never to set foot in Salt Lake again, not until the Mormon Church relented and went back to following God's revelation about polygamy."

The old man leaned to one side so that he could reach the back pocket of his work pants. The wallet he brought out was as old and worn as he was. He opened it carefully, extracted a folded newspaper clipping, and gave it to Traveler.

The article was half a page wide. Centered in the middle was a photograph of a man identified as Clarence Eldredge. Clustered around him were half a dozen women; his wives, according to the caption. All of them wore homespun dresses and old-fashioned sunbonnets.

Traveler scanned the article to refresh his memory. Clarence Eldredge had made national news five years ago by getting himself murdered. At the time his eldest son, Zeke, had been charged with patricide but was eventually acquitted. Testimony at the trial varied from one extreme to the other. Some witnesses claimed that no murder had taken place, that it was solely a church matter of blood atonement, Zeke having killed his father to free the old man of sin, one of Brigham Young's favorite prescriptions. Others said it was justifiable homicide, because Clarence had tried to steal away his son's younger wives. In any case, Zeke disappeared after the trial, taking with him two brothers and his father's wives, among them a woman named in the article as Priscilla Eldredge.

"How many Eldredges are there?" Traveler asked.

"That's a good question. When Zeke surfaced again in Glory, he had women with him, but no brothers. Some say they took off on their own, forming their own religions. Others say the desert in southern Utah is full of unmarked graves. Which brings me to the point. With his record, Zeke Eldredge is the one the police should have arrested."

"It might be a good idea if you gave this article to Pepper's lawyer when he gets one."

"He's got one already." The old man delved into his wallet again and came out with a cream-colored business card, which he handed to Traveler.

The card felt expensive. Its texture reminded Traveler of heavy parchment. The named embossed on it, SAMUEL J. HOWE, ATTORNEY AT LAW, conveyed more than money.

"How the hell did he get Sam Howe?"

Kilgore exposed his palms, gesturing ignorance. "He just sort of showed up at the jail when I was trying to get in to see Pepper."

"He's one of the top criminal lawyers in town. I understand he's on permanent retainer to the church. A hired gunslinger waiting in the wings to shoot down trouble."

"What kind of trouble?"

Traveler shrugged. "Is Pepper a member of the church?"

"Not as far as I know."

Traveler returned the newspaper clipping and the calling card. "This may be a waste of time, you coming to me. Attorneys usually do the hiring when it comes to private detectives."

The old man shook his head adamantly. "I'm the one Pepper trusts. He asked *me* to get help."

"I can't get in to see Pepper without his attorney's permission."

"Does that mean you're going to work for us?"

Traveler slumped against the booth's red plastic backrest and closed his eyes. The old Bees were there waiting for him, Ted Ingram at first base, Bob Allen at second, and Pepper at shortstop. But third base eluded his memory, as did left and right field. Center, though, was visible. That belonged to Chuck Cecil, the only Bee to make it to the big leagues. Pete Watson was behind the plate as usual, having a hell of a time digging Kilgore's spitters out of the dirt.

"Have you kept in touch with any of the old team?" he asked when he opened his eyes.

"I had a note from Chuck Cecil a while back. You remember him, don't you?"

Traveler nodded.

"A dead pull hitter, Chuck was. If we'd had a short porch for him here at Derks, he would have hit fifty home runs for us. It was a damned shame he ended up at St. Louis, with those long fences. It cut his career short, not being able to hit to the opposite field. Still, a year on top is better than nothing. Chuck lives in California now, Orange County. He's some kind of a salesman."

Kilgore was staring out the window again, searching for better times. When tickets to the Bees games were ninety cents. Malted milks a quarter. And Sloan's Liniment was standing by in the bull pen.

"I tried to buy one of Chuck's bubble gum cards a while back. I couldn't afford it. The damn things are worth a small fortune these days." The old man's shoulders sagged. "That says it all, doesn't it? God, what I wouldn't give to go back thirty years. Money was worth something then."

Traveler shook his head to indicate he preferred the present, where his fee was two hundred and fifty dollars a day, not twenty-five.

"I still feel like the same man." Gingerly Kilgore fingered his protruding stomach. "Except for my weight. But you should see Chuck Cecil. He must weigh close to two-fifty. As for the rest of my boys, I don't know where they are. Why do you ask anyway?"

"Curiosity, that's all."

"You still haven't answered my question, Mo. Are you working for us or not?"

The answer had been inevitable from the moment he heard Hap Kilgore's voice on the phone.

"I charge twenty-five dollars a day, Hap."

When the old man's eyes widened, Traveler added, "That includes mileage of course."

"It's Pepper's money we're trying to save. Just remember that. In the meantime, I'll try to come up with something for you."

"If I can't do you any good in the next couple of days, I'll take a walk. No charge."

What Traveler didn't say was that he might be off the case long before that. The police weren't about to invite his help on a murder case, not with the likes of Zeke Eldredge in the background. And if the church decided to clamp down, then twenty-five dollars a day would be overcharging for all the good Traveler could do.

"We're not asking for charity," Kilgore said.

"I know that."

"Just so you do." Kilgore patted his wallet pocket. "I know a retainer is customary, but all I've got on me at the moment is bus fare."

"Where were you planning to go?"

"Ever since the wife died, I've had a room at the Phoebe Clinton out on Twelfth East."

"Come on," Traveler said, suddenly unable to look the old man in the eye. "I'll drive you."

Its full name was the Phoebe Clinton Home for the Aged. It had been a landmark since before Traveler was born.

5

THE PHOEBE CLINTON HOME took up an entire city block. It sat back far enough from the street to allow a circular driveway, one that had been patched so many times over the years that it resembled a jigsaw puzzle. The freshly painted house, three stories in the center with two-story wings on either side, had been built in the 1880s by one of Utah's silver kings. It was said to be a replica of a stately home he'd seen while vacationing in England. He'd added his own Utah touches, of course, like the Gothic columns out front that held up an elaborately corniced, gargoyle-friezed porte cochere.

When Traveler's Ford pulled under the overhang, Kilgore made a clucking sound with his tongue and turned his baseball cap around like a catcher. "I've never come in this way before. Usually it's reserved for important guests. Sometimes ambulances, depending on who's riding inside. There's a side door for hired help like me. Residents are asked to use it, too, to keep from tracking dirt into the entrance hall. Hearses come and go by the back door."

"Where do private detectives fit in?"

The old man snorted. "Mother Mary will have a conniption fit if she sees either one of us out here."

"I figured the place to be Mormon, not Catholic."

"It's neither one." Kilgore opened the gym bag on his lap, feeling around inside until he found a pouch of Redman tobacco. He loaded one cheek to abscess proportions before continuing. "Her name's really Mary Cook. Some of the old-timers around here call her Mother Mary because she treats them like children."

He got out of the car, keeping his back to the house. One side of his face contorted into a conspirator's wink just before he fired a blob of tobacco juice onto the patchwork driveway.

"Don't call me here," he said. "There's no damned privacy on the phone."

Without waiting for an answer, Kilgore turned and walked toward the side of the house. Halfway there, his shoulders slumped, as if his gym bag had suddenly become an intolerable burden. His walk had slowed to a shuffle by the time he turned the corner and disappeared.

On impulse Traveler followed him. He sprinted to the side of the building. From that vantage point, he watched the old man pass by a side door and continue along a crumbling concrete walkway that closely paralleled the house. The side of the house, unlike the front, looked like it hadn't been painted in decades. A toolshed stood at the rear of the structure. Beyond that was a half-acre garden dominated by weeds and scraggly rosebushes that had yet to flower.

Kilgore entered the toolshed and closed the door behind him without once looking back.

Traveler stood there for a moment, captured by the view of the Wasatch Mountains beyond the garden. Clouds had broken free of the peaks at last. Plumes of moisture trailed from the leading thunderhead.

He took a deep breath, wondering what the hell he was doing there, then hurried along the pavement to the side entrance. A glass storm door, one of those models that converted to a screen door in warm weather, blocked his way with rusty security bars camouflaged as scrollwork.

A button was mounted on the door frame, along with a sign that read RING FOR DELIVERIES. He did. The bell echoed a long time. He was about to ring again when a heavyset woman came lumbering down a linoleumed corridor toward him. She was wearing a nurse's uniform white enough to dazzle his eyes. When she reached the door, sunlight reflecting off the material forced him to squint.

She squinted back and said, "Is that your car out front?"

"I left it there when I dropped off Mr. Kilgore."

Her grim squint dissolved into a smile. The expression made her cheeks look like puckered bread dough. "That was kind of you, Mr. . . ."

"Traveler," he supplied.

She opened the door and joined him on the cement stoop outside. The plastic name tag over her heart said she was Mrs. Cook. Mother Mary. "We appreciate any help given to our residents here, Mr. Traveler. You see, most of them are not allowed to drive."

"Because of their age?"

"For one thing. But we really don't have the parking. We're located in a residential area, as you can see for yourself. As it is, we've already had complaints about staff members taking up all the available spaces in the neighborhood."

"I'll move my car."

"There's no hurry now that I know who it belongs to."

"I wanted to ask you about Mr. Kilgore."

"He still drives," she said, misunderstanding the intent of his question. "Hap is one of our younger residents, you know. He even drives our seniors' van on occasion. There for a while he used to get extra free tickets to the Saints baseball games. Whenever he did, he'd make it a regular outing for some of our more sports-minded residents. Naturally, there was always a staff member on hand to supervise. I—"

Her lips pressed together as she bit off the word. "What am I thinking of? I'm sure you didn't come here to listen to me rattle on about our problems. Now, if there's anything else?"

"Actually, I'm here because Mr. Kilgore has asked me to help him."

One hand went to her heart, like someone about to recite the Pledge of Allegiance.

"I hope there isn't any trouble," she said.

Traveler would have preferred not to identify himself at the moment, since that might embarrass his client. On the other hand, word of his talk with Mother Mary would probably get back to Hap anyway.

He handed her a business card.

"My God, why would he need a detective?"

"It's nothing to do with the home here, Mrs. Cook, I assure you. It's an old friend that Hap's worried about."

She sighed with relief and handed back the card. "And I suppose you want to know if Mr. Kilgore can pay?"

He nodded, though that wasn't what he'd had in mind.

"Mr. Kilgore does a little janitorial work and gardening for us. It's make-work really. He likes to keep busy and we oblige him. He often tells people that he's an employee of the home. Actually he's our youngest full-time resident. Whatever work he does is strictly voluntary, with no pay attached."

"I—"

She overrode him. "We've found from experience, Mr. Traveler, that it's best if our residents don't carry money. You see, people tend to take advantage of the elderly. Naturally, Mr. Kilgore gets spending money for bus fare and the like. That being the case, you'll probably be leaving now."

"Would you happen to know Pepper Dalton?"

The woman tilted her head to one side and then the other. "What is it you really want, Mr. Traveler?"

"To help Hap."

At that moment, the sunshine disappeared, erased by the thunderhead racing west toward the Great Salt Lake. The temperature dropped dramatically.

Mrs. Cook hugged herself. Gooseflesh pimpled her heavy arms.

"Now about Pepper Dalton," he prompted.

"That's Mr. Kilgore's baseball friend. I met him once. I don't know anything else about him."

"Did you ever see Hap Kilgore play ball?"

"Why is it that men fantasize about their youth when they grow old? Every day Mr. Kilgore goes off to that baseball park of his. He takes the bus and even has to transfer. And why?"

Traveler shrugged.

"So he can pretend to be young again."

He closed his eyes and saw Hap taking the mound, red-faced and reeking of Sloan's Liniment, windmilling his arm to get the fastball ready.

"Women are too realistic to waste their time on such things, Mr. Traveler. Now, if you'll excuse me. It's getting cold out here."

He opened his eyes in time to see the first rain fall. She blinked at him and retreated inside, locking the storm door behind her.

He ran for the Ford.

6

BY THE TIME TRAVELER drove downtown the spring storm had turned into a cloudburst. Gutters were overflowing onto the sidewalks. Pedestrians were huddled under awnings and in doorways. His Ford was one of the few cars on South Temple Street.

When he reached the Chester Building—three stories of granite and sandstone that mixed Victorian, Art Deco and fervor into a kind of Utah Gothic—there wasn't a soul in sight. Even the temple tourists across the street had taken shelter, presumably in the Tabernacle, where, on a weekday, the best they could hope for was canned choir music.

The ten-yard dash to the building's bronze revolving doors left him soaked. He dripped all the way across the marble floor to the cigar counter where Barney Chester, the building's owner, was lighting a cheroot in his eternal flame. As soon as he had his cigar going, he pointed it at the WPA fresco of Brigham Young on the ceiling and said, "If you're heading up to your office, you'll have to walk."

"Where's Nephi?"

"Eighty miles south of Salt Lake where it's always been," Chester wisecracked. He was a short, wiry man with dark, curly hair who looked vaguely like Edward G. Robinson. The resemblance, he contended, had left him almost as scarred as seeing *Bambi* as a child.

"Nephi Bates," Traveler said, refusing to acknowledge the town of that name. "Your elevator operator. Named for the son of Lehi in *The Book of Mormon*."

"Oh, him." Chester rolled the cigar along his lips, wetting it down. "He's across the street attending a baptism for the dead."

Traveler grimaced. That made twice in the last week.

"I know how you feel," Chester said. "A delegation from the church was in here trying to convince me that the ceremony qualified as a legitimate religious holiday. You know me. I threw them out."

Traveler knew him all right. Chester loved playing iconoclast, but he'd never say or do anything to hurt a true believer.

"I told them I'd dock Nephi's pay. Otherwise, he'd be taking time off to baptize every one of his ancestors into heaven, all the way back to Adam."

Traveler held up his hands in surrender. "I'm not up to it today, Barney."

Chester dismissed the capitulation by leaning nonchalantly against one of two Doric columns that sandwiched the cigar counter. "The poor bastard has to stand in the baptismal font once for each and every relative. On a day like this, you'd think he'd have sense enough to stand out in the rain and get his baptisms straight from heaven."

"Rain's polluted."

Chewing on his cigar, Chester screwed up one side of his face. Instead of looking like a gangster, he reminded Traveler of Bambi's pal, Thumper.

"Mo," he said at last, "you look properly baptized yourself."

Traveler's wet Levis were chafing his thighs. His shirt

was stuck to his back, and his Reeboks made squishing noises when he walked. "How about running me up to my office?"

"The elevator's in the basement with Bill and Charlie."

"It's not like you to trust them with it."

"Charlie's making a few adjustments to the phone lines." He led Traveler around the column to point at the shelf that usually held the coffee urn. In its place stood a compact computer, complete with printer and phone hookup. "He says he knows a way to save me line charges."

"You ought to know better."

Chester poked himself in the chest with his thumb. "Hey, it's the computer that makes the calls. Not me. Besides which, Charlie tells me I can depreciate the whole thing if I use the computer for inventory control."

Traveler glanced at the glass display case. The Bull Durham, Sen-Sen and Chiclets were as faded and dusty as ever.

"Charlie said that?"

"Not exactly. Bill was paraphrasing him."

Traveler shook his head. "Are you telling me that the computer is Charlie's idea?"

"I've been thinking about getting one for a long time," Chester said, though his tone lacked conviction. "He and Bill helped me make up my mind, that's all."

Charlie Redwine, a full-blooded Navajo, was the one and only disciple of Boyd "Mad Bill" Williams, known as Salt Lake's Sandwich Prophet.

"What happened to the coffeepot?" Traveler asked.

"It's around the corner in the men's room. Charlie said we couldn't plug it in to the same outlet or we'd blow the circuit."

Without another word, Traveler stepped into the public rest room. The coffee, though perking, couldn't compete with the smell of deodorant coming from the urinals. Holding his breath, he carried a cup back into the lobby and tried smelling it there. But by then his nose had ceased to function properly. He was about to complain when he heard the elevator cables start to sing. He and Barney walked over to greet the rising elevator.

The lift's bronze grillwork was Art Deco from the 1920s like much of the Chester Building. Even before the door opened Mad Bill was touching thumb and forefinger together in a signal of success. Charlie raised one palm, like a movie Indian. Today, he was wearing a fringed serape that looked more K mart than Navajo. Bill wore one of his sandwich boards. It bore his own brand of scripture: TITHING ACCEPTED HERE.

"We're all set for a demonstration," he announced the moment he stepped out of the elevator. Without waiting for a response, he led the way back to the cigar counter, his prophet's robes flapping around his ankles.

Traveler followed out of curiosity. As soon as he joined Bill and Chester on the spectators' side of the display case, Charlie rolled a rickety chair up to the computer and sat down.

"He's testing the phone setup," Bill explained, ducking out from under his sandwich board and storing it to one side. "It's called a modem. It lets us talk to other computers."

Barney rolled his cigar between his fingers and looked thoughtful. "What's important here, Mo, is that Charlie says we can tap into the church computer."

"Why, for God's sake?"

"To see if Nephi Bates is a church spy, of course."

"Amen," Bill said. "Though it's really not necessary, because I can feel it in my soul. The man has been sent among us for one purpose only: to keep track of me and my emerging religion."

Traveler silenced a groan by sipping his coffee. The taste set his teeth on edge. "A spy wouldn't slip church literature under my door every day."

"That's just what a spy would want you to think."

"Barney hired him, not the church," Traveler reminded them before abandoning his cup on the countertop.

"He was willing to work cheap," Bill said. "That's suspicious right there."

The Indian grunted for attention. His fingers flew over the keyboard. Data appeared on the amber screen.

"Where did he learn that?" Traveler asked no one in particular. He knew better than to direct questions at Charlie, who seldom said anything other than "How," and then with derision. As for the Navajo's education, all Traveler knew was that it had ended at Brigham Young University when the worship of peyote got him expelled. After that, he'd been a typical, bottle-a-day West Temple Indian before taking up with Mad Bill.

"When God sent Charles to me," the Sandwich Prophet answered, "he came filled with the knowledge necessary to be first disciple of the Church of the True Prophet."

Traveler rolled his eyes and thought about the change of clothes he had upstairs. His shoulders twitched in a vain attempt to escape the damp workshirt clinging to his back. "The Mormon Church has the tightest security in the world."

When Traveler started for the elevator, Barney caught hold of his arm and dragged him back. "Charlie's been working on this all morning. We're damn near in."

"Have faith, Mo," Bill said. "Hackers broke into the computers at Los Alamos."

"Atomic secrets are one thing, church security quite another."

"Charlie's already been into the university's computer."

"He gave Bill a Ph.D. in comparative religion," Barney added.

The Sandwich Prophet took a deep breath, expanding his chest to almost the size of his stomach. "How about it, Mo? Would you like a college degree at last?"

Inside, Traveler winced. Four years playing football at USC had earned him two years' worth of credits.

Barney released his hold on Traveler's arm to gesture expansively. "What about me? I could use a little education."

Charlie grunted.

"He's on the verge," Bill translated.

The name Nephi Bates appeared on the screen, along with the notation that he was a member in good standing. Additional data were available upon coded request.

"That means more work," Bill explained as the Indian began hitting keys again. "But that proves it as far as I'm concerned. The man's a spy."

Barney nodded without taking his eyes from the computer screen.

"Jesus," Traveler muttered, and headed for the elevator. Halfway there, he paused to add, "The FBI is going to get you, one way or another."

He knew, like the rest of them did, that J. Edgar Hoover's Catholic-dominated FBI had been infiltrated by Mormons in recent years. In fact, there were those who suspected premeditation on the part of the church, since ex-agents now ran the LDS security system.

"On second thought," he said, returning to the cigar counter, "they might not have the newest phone-tracing equipment. Not yet anyway."

Abruptly Barney stopped chewing on his cigar and stepped back far enough from the counter to have a clear view of the front entrance. His tough-guy expression dissolved into one of apprehension. "I never thought about that." He tugged at the sleeve of Bill's robe. "Maybe we'd better back off for a while. I mean, there's no hurry, is there, now that we know how to get in?"

Before Bill had time to respond, Traveler said, "Run another name for me, will you, Charlie? Rick Dalton. Nicknamed Pepper."

The Indian glanced at his prophet, seeking approval. Bill gave it with a twitchy nod.

Charlie keyed in the request. The name came up, along with the notations to see Jessie Gilchrist and the Deseret Coal and Gas Company.

"Now Gilchrist."

On screen, Gilchrist was listed as vice president and general manager of the Salt Lake Saints baseball team.

Traveler was about to run Golly Simpson when a siren sounded outside in the street. An instant later the revolving door hissed into action.

"Shit," Barney said. "Close her down."

In one motion Charlie switched off the power and pulled the serape over his head and onto the computer.

Traveler's father came dripping across the slippery marble floor to say, "I had a hell of a time getting here. Half the streets are flooded. There are accidents all over town. The police are going crazy out there." He had a wet paper bag under his arm.

"Damn," the Indian said, uncovering the equipment.

Bill pointed a finger at Martin. "Were you followed?"

"By whom?"

"Danites, of course."

Martin looked at his son, widened his eyes, and sighed. In the early days of Mormonism Joseph Smith and Brigham Young had created their own secret police force known as the Danites. Their job was to keep the faithful in line and outsiders—or Gentiles, as Mormons called everyone besides themselves—in their place. Some said the Danites still existed, though Traveler thought it more likely that their functions had been usurped by the church's high-tech, FBI-inspired security system.

The computer beeped as Charlie switched it back on.

"They've broken into the church's computer system," Traveler said for his father's benefit. "They're trying to check up on Nephi Bates."

"Why not just hire another elevator operator?" Martin said.

"They'd just replace him," Barney answered.

Martin winked at his son. "Hire a relative, for God's sake."

Bill signaled for silence. "Nephi is a fringe benefit only. What we're seeking here is truth. Proof that the church is conspiring against me and my Church of the True Prophet."

"That's the first I've heard of it," Barney said. "If I'd known that, I'd never have put up the money for a computer."

Bill held up a hand. "Render therefore unto Caesar the things which are Caesar's; and unto God the things that are God's."

"Matthew, twenty-two, twenty-one," the Indian said, struggling back into his serape. His voice, Traveler noticed, sounded vaguely like Bill's.

"What Charlie means is that worldly uses of the computer are yours, Barney." Bill cocked his head as if listening to inner voices. "Holy uses are something else again."

Another siren sounded in the distance.

"That's it," Barney said, slipping behind the counter to pull the plug. "It's my phone line you're using." He looked to Traveler for moral support.

Martin held out his paper bag. "I've got a fresh jug in here."

Bill and Charlie beat Martin and Traveler to the elevator, which was old-fashioned enough to have a start-stop handle instead of buttons. The Indian lowered a retractable operator's seat from a recess in the wall and settled onto it.

"Floor, please?" Bill said.

Martin pointed up.

"Three it is," Bill said. The elevator bucked once before

rising. Barney waved at them through the open grillwork and then picked up the computer. He was heading toward the men's room when the second floor intervened and they lost sight of him.

7

THE OFFICE OF MORONI TRAVELER & SON was on the third and top floor of the Chester Building, a corner room with windows looking out onto the temple to the north and the Wasatch Mountains to the east. Among other things it contained two wooden desks placed back-to-back, filing cabinets, a couple of small tables and four client's chairs, though there had never been occasion to use that many at once.

Martin deposited the wine bottle on his son's desk, then took up his usual position, hands clasped behind his back as he stood at the northern window staring out at the temple across the street. From the tilt of Martin's head, Traveler knew his father was studying the Angel Moroni, whose golden statue graced the temple's tallest spire. Beyond the angel, blue sky showed in the wake of thunderheads moving west toward the lake. The rain had stopped.

Traveler picked up the wine jug and unscrewed its cap.

"Praise the Lord and pass the ammunition," Bill said, taking the jug from Traveler.

"Amen," Charlie mouthed before dipping into a filing cabinet and coming out with a stack of plastic cups, which he quickly separated into a line of four on Traveler's desk.

Bill poured carefully, filling each cup to within a half inch of its brim. The moment he finished Charlie dug beneath his serape and pulled a Bull Durham pouch from his shirt pocket. He extracted a pinch of something and sprinkled it over two of the cups.

"Peyote for religious purposes is legal for Indians," Bill explained.

Charlie held his pouch over one of the other cups and looked expectantly at Traveler.

"Nothing for me. I can't go out into the land of Zion with liquor on my breath."

Bill grinned. "'Strong drinks are not for the belly, but for the washing of your bodies.' That's Doctrine and Covenants, Mo. The word of God, in Joe's Smith's ear and out his mouth. But I say people must wash inside and out." He drained his cup, as did his disciple.

Martin turned from the sunlit window to say, "Why don't you take the bottle with you, men? I'm sure Barney would like a drink."

"You will always have a place of honor in the Church of the True Prophet." Bill held the half-gallon bottle up to the light coming from the window. "Isn't that true, Charlie?"

The Indian, whose eyes had begun to glaze, jerked his head. It could have been a nod or a twitch.

"Come, Charles, these men have work to do. So do we."

Bill took the Indian by the arm and led him from the office. Halfway down the hall they began singing "Onward Christian Soldiers."

Martin went back to gazing out the window.

"I want to thank you for sending Hap Kilgore my way," Traveler said to his father's back.

"I'm too old to get mixed up in murder."

"He's your friend, Dad."

Martin denied it with a single shake of his head. "I remember the day you got his autograph at Derks Field."

"You were a Bees fan, too."

"Kilgore was more your mother's friend than mine."

The last sentence had been delivered in a tone so neutral there had to be hidden meaning. The set of his father's shoulders confirmed as much.

"You're forgetting that I'm retired," he said.

"Sure. Those missing persons cases of yours are merely a hobby."

Martin swung around. Sunlight haloed his head, making his face impossible to read. "Friend or no friend, Kilgore was one hell of a talker. He could tell jokes all night, one after the other. Most of them dirty, too. He had a trick of spitting tobacco just before the punch line, if location permitted. Women seemed to love him."

Martin snorted at his memory. "Those were the days when your mother and I used to hang out at the Zang. That's where we met him, you know."

Nodding, Traveler thought of Hap Kilgore as he'd seen him less than an hour ago. The vision didn't fit with Martin's recollection.

"He was quite a clown in the locker room, too," his father went on. "I guess it was his way of building rapport with his players. It worked—they played their guts out for him."

"Exactly how did you meet him?" Traveler asked, hoping to elicit more about his mother's relationship with Kilgore.

"Speaking of women," Martin said, as if reading his son's mind, "Claire called."

Traveler took a breath before asking, "What did she want?"

"Nothing special. The usual threats."

8

THE CHANGE OF CLOTHES Traveler kept in the office closet
was intended for business meetings, not rain emergen-
cies. The gray slacks felt tight and restrictive, as did
the charcoal sport coat with its herringbone pattern.
The white broadcloth shirt with button-down collar
choked him when he tightened the tie with its regimental
stripes.

"Are you going after Claire?" Martin asked from behind his desk.

"I have a client, in case you've forgotten."

"Hap Kilgore is your hero, not mine." Martin left the
shelter of his desk. "I'm going to rescue that bottle of
wine."

"Knowing Bill and Charlie, it's already too late."

"Then I'll find my own, because it's time to get
drunk."

"And your missing persons?"

"Sooner or later everybody gets lost."

"Before you do too, I want to know if we have any
markers owed us by the police department."

"Nothing to cover murder," Martin said as he left the
office.

Traveler stared at the door for a while, half expecting

his father to return with still another last word. Only when he heard the elevator door open and close did he pick up the phone and dial the police.

Sergeant Aldon Rasmussen, a part-time dealer in sports memorabilia who'd sold bits and pieces of Traveler's past, was out of the office. So Traveler ended up talking to Anson Horne, a lieutenant attached to the chief's office for press and church liaison. The nature of Horne's job and his personality matched perfectly. Gentiles were the enemy. Gentiles and private detectives. Traveler belonged to both categories.

"Just the man I wanted to talk to," Horne said without a trace of his usual sarcasm.

"Yes," Traveler said warily.

"I have a bet with somebody here in the office about you."

"Yes?"

"I say professional linebackers like hurting people. Like the gazooney you crippled for life. I say you loved it. But my friend says all that business about pro football players and their wild-eyed play is just so much TV hype. What do you say, Moroni?"

That you're a son of a bitch, Traveler thought. Out loud he said, "I'll trade you an answer for information."

"You must want something badly."

"And you?"

"I want your soul, Moroni. Failing that, your ass. Now what do you want?"

Traveler hesitated, wondering if he should even bother with a Gentile-baiter like Horne. But what harm could it do?

"I want to see Pepper Dalton," Traveler said.

"No deal. I really wanted you to owe me one, too." With that the cop hung up.

Traveler made another call directly to the watch commander at the jail. As expected, he was informed, politely, that Dalton's lawyer of record was Samuel Howe. Permission to see the prisoner was strictly up to him.

Traveler decided to make one last try, a call to Howe's office. Surprise. His secretary said she'd be glad to squeeze him in for an appointment. One hour from now, right after Mr. Howe's late lunch.

9

THE ELEVATOR WAS HALFWAY to the lobby when Traveler heard voices chanting from below. "To Zion pull the handcart, while singing every day. The glorious songs of Zion that haste the time away."

His great-grandmother had pulled a handcart across the Mormon trail, from Council Bluffs, Iowa, over the Rocky Mountains and all the way to Utah. The daguerreotypes of her showed a small, frail woman weighing not much more than a hundred pounds.

"We climb the hills and far away, then down where sleeping valleys lay, while still the miles onward roll. Till Zion rises on our sight, we pull our handcarts with our might."

The singing stopped when the elevator reached ground level. Through the grillwork Traveler saw Martin and Barney standing behind the cigar counter, arm-in-arm. Their faces were flushed with wine. Bill and Charlie were nowhere to be seen.

Traveler stepped out into the lobby and looked around. Interpreting Traveler's glance, Barney said, "Our brothers have gone out into the land of Zion seeking donations for their church." It was his way of referring to Bill and Charlie's technique of panhandling.

Traveler said, "I think you two had better get some food inside you."

"I can't leave my post," Barney said, lighting a fresh cigar. He blew smoke rings at the fresco of Brigham Young overhead. They dissipated long before reaching the thirty-foot ceiling.

Martin disappeared behind the counter long enough to retrieve the empty wine jug. "Go not into the land of Zion with liquor on your breath."

"Sen-Sen erases all sin," Barney answered.

"What about guilt?" Martin picked up.

Traveler stepped around the counter and took his father by the arm.

"And a child shall lead them," Barney said.

"Toward the promised land," Martin added.

Shaking his head, Traveler hustled his father across the lobby and out through the bronze revolving door. New thunderheads, fresh from their spawning ground in the Wasatch Mountains, filled the sky.

Rain drove the two men into the Grabeteria just around the corner on Main Street. As usual they ate roast beef sandwiches standing up, their cafeteria-style trays resting on the chest-high counter in front of the plate-glass window that faced out onto Main. From that vantage point, Martin insisted he could identify Mormons going in and out of the ZCMI across the street. If they squirmed, he contended, they were in search of new *Garments*, the holy underwear the faithful were required to wear at all times.

Up the street to their left, Brigham Young's statue stood in the middle of the intersection where South Temple Street met Main. He gleamed in the rain.

Traveler closed his eyes to concentrate on chewing.

When he opened them a shaft of sunlight had escaped the clouds to probe the face of the ZCMI. The ray moved like a searchlight trying to pick out targets.

"I brought your mother here to eat once," Martin said, suddenly sounding none the worse for wine. "But only once. She thought they were fools to run this place on the honor system."

The shaft of sunlight headed up the street toward the prophet.

"She cheated on the tab but didn't tell me until we were halfway home. I came back later and paid. When she found out about it, she said I was the fool."

Traveler glanced at the antique trolley bell, complete with rope pull, that was mounted on the wall behind the cash register. They rang it whenever a customer was caught cheating.

When he looked out the window again, Brigham Young was caught in sunlight.

"There are times when Claire reminds me of your mother," Martin went on.

Traveler's swallow grew sharp edges that hurt his throat.

"Hearing her voice on the phone today brought it all back. The kind of games women play."

Tone of voice gave his father away. There'd been more to Claire's message than had been reported.

Traveler took a sip of water. It, too, went down hard. "All right, Dad. Let's have it."

"I didn't want to speak in front of Bill and Charlie back in the office."

"And when they left?"

Martin raised his shoulders and kept them there, up near his ears as if to ward off a chill. "You have Hap Kilgore to worry about."

"You don't need to protect me."

Martin's shoulders drooped back to where they'd been.

He turned his head slowly in Traveler's direction. "That's what parents are for."

Without warning, Traveler hugged his father.

"For Christ's sake, Moroni, you're going to make me spill my food." Martin pulled out of his son's grasp and looked around as if embarrassed.

"Quit stalling," Traveler said.

Martin sighed. "Claire said she has a new kind of game to play with you."

"What kind?"

"That she didn't say."

Traveler stuffed half a sandwich into his mouth and began chewing methodically. Claire's first games had been in bed.

"Women," Martin breathed. "You don't see me getting married again, do you?"

Traveler's only answer was to chew harder.

"When Kary, your mother, died I said to myself, 'You're past it anyway. You don't have to be led around by your balls anymore.'"

He looked around for eavesdroppers. When he found none he continued. "The trouble is, the sap still rises once in a while."

Traveler swallowed and clenched his teeth.

"When that happens I get drunk. That's just as good as sex at my age. But at yours?" Martin's head shook. "You've got to find someone else to play games with."

"I haven't seen Claire in months."

"You should see the look on your face."

Traveler studied the window in front of him, but it was free of reflection. The only thing revealed was blue sky.

"The storm's breaking up again," he said.

"Good," his father answered. "Because I've got a date."

"You know what happens to sap in the spring."

Martin grinned. "A plane has my name on it at the airport."

His father had learned to fly during the war and had kept up his license ever since, including a full instrument rating for single-engine aircraft. Traveler had yet to go up with him.

"There are those who say flying gets them closer to God," Martin said.

"Just the two of you up there, is that right?"

Martin winked. "I owe a lot to the army."

The details of Martin's service were unclear, since he refused to talk about the war, a situation that had made Kary furious.

"Your father came home a hero," she had said every time the subject came up. "A band was playing and there he was with a chestful of medals. But I never believed a word of it. If he'd been a real hero, he would have bragged about it like everyone else."

10

SAMUEL HOWE AND ASSOCIATES occupied the tenth and top floor of the Kearns Building on Main Street between First and Second South. It was within easy walking distance for Traveler, who arrived five minutes early for his appointment. Since he knew they'd probably keep him waiting anyway, he stood outside for a while, enjoying the rain-freshened air and admiring the building, one of Salt Lake's landmarks.

The Kearns had been constructed in 1911 for Thomas Kearns, one of the mining millionaires to come out of Park City in the 1880s. Its reinforced concrete was a marvel of the time, as was a design hinting at a Renaissance revival that included terra-cotta tile, brick veneer and bold cornices.

Kearns, like his building, became a fixture in Utah. Although a Catholic, he served one term in the United States Senate, taking office at the turn of the century, a time when a kind of gentleman's agreement existed between church and Gentiles. One senator would be LDS, the church decreed, and one would be a Gentile, a policy to placate Mormon-baiters in Washington.

Traveler took a deep breath. A breeze coming off the mountains carried with it the smell of pine and sage. It reminded him of childhood outings he'd taken with his father at Rockwell's Flats, an area of Cottonwood Canyon since bulldozed for ski resorts.

What would Tom Kearns think of his city today? Traveler wondered as he walked into a lobby far less grand than the Chester Building's. The Kearns's elevator was in better shape, though, with buttons to push instead of the likes of Nephi Bates at the controls.

Carpet that smelled like old money led Traveler across the tenth-floor foyer to an elegant antique desk, behind which sat an even more elegant receptionist. The highly polished metal plaque said his name was Mr. VanHorn. Behind him were two impressively paneled oak doors, both closed.

"Moroni Traveler to see Mr. Howe."

"Someone will be with you in a moment, sir." He pushed a button on his phone console.

A minute or so later one of the doors opened. The man who stepped through it was short, no more than five-five. He had close-cropped sandy hair with bushy eyebrows to match. His white shirtsleeves were rolled to his elbows; his collar was unbuttoned and his tie hung loose. He shook

hands fiercely, as if to prove himself against Traveler's bulk.

"Sam Howe," he said. "I've always wanted to meet you." With a brusque gesture he indicated that Traveler was to follow him through the open door.

The same carpet continued into the wide corridor beyond. They passed half a dozen heavy doors, including one with gold lettering that said SAMUEL HOWE. When Traveler stopped in front of it, Howe kept on going toward a door at the end of the hall, over which glowed a discreet Exit sign.

The man retraced his steps to Traveler's side. "On a day like this, Moroni—you don't mind if I call you Moroni, do you?—it's best to enjoy God's fresh air at every opportunity."

"Mr. Howe, I've been hired to help Pepper Dalton. In order to do that, I need to see him."

The lawyer nodded. "Follow me, Moroni."

Without waiting for an answer Howe continued down the hall to the exit door. When he opened it, bright daylight flooded the short flight of steps that led up to the roof. From there, they could see the entire valley. To the west, the Great Salt Lake looked as blue as the ocean. To the east, the Wasatch Mountains had been covered with fresh snow and seemed close enough to touch in the shimmering air. Still another procession of thunderheads, blacker even than those before them, loomed above the 10,000-foot peaks.

"At times like this," Howe said, "I know Salt Lake is the most beautiful place in the world. But then I see it differently from most people. I wasn't born here."

"I need your permission to see Pepper Dalton," Traveler persisted.

"I haven't decided if we need the services of a private detective as yet."

"I'm working for one of Pepper's friends."

"Of course you are, Moroni. But that's your business. My business is to look after the interests of my client."

"They're one and the same," Traveler said, but couldn't help wondering which client Howe had in mind. He was, after all, the church's thirteenth and unnamed apostle. As such, he could give the appearance of being unbiased, even pro-Gentile when it suited him.

"Look around you, Moroni." Howe made a sweeping gesture meant to encompass the entire valley. "Since moving here, I've studied Salt Lake's history. Think of what it took to build this city. The guts, the faith. This was nothing more than a wasteland when Brigham Young led his people here. And what did they find? I'll tell you. Not very much. Even the Indians had little use for this valley. They only came here to harvest crickets when they got desperate for food. But Brigham took one look at it and said, 'This is the place.'"

Howe's head shook as if he couldn't believe his own words. "His promised land, his Eden. Think of it. Quite probably this was the most hostile environment ever to face American pioneers. And Brigham Young turned it into the crossroads of the West."

"You argue a good case. I hope you do as well for Pepper."

"I never discuss my clients, or their cases, in advance of the trial."

"From what I hear, the church is your client."

The lawyer squinted at Traveler, then turned suddenly to point north. "Look at the temple. Even a Gentile like you would have to call that a monument to faith."

At the top of one of the spires the golden Angel Moroni shimmered as if it had caught fire in the sunlight.

"It took forty years to build. Ox teams hauled granite blocks one at a time from Little Cottonwood Canyon. That's twenty miles away. Think of it. Think of the dedication. It was pioneers like that who made this country what it is today."

"You're quite a convert."

"There's hope for everyone, Moroni."

"I understand that Pepper is a Gentile."

"I was a Gentile once. I saw the light."

"A Gentile without money if he's convicted," Traveler added.

"My client is innocent. When I prove that in court, he'll come into his inheritance, both financial and spiritual."

"Why would a man like you involve yourself in a murder case?"

The lawyer smiled. "I'm a good friend to have, Moroni."

"And a bad enemy. Is that what you're saying?"

"In this town you don't want to step on the wrong toes."

Traveler glanced at Howe's perfectly polished shoes. "Church toes, I take it."

Howe looked down at Traveler's scuffed loafers and shook his head.

"I don't understand why the church is involved in this," Traveler said. "My God, polygamists and murder. That's just the kind of publicity they don't want."

"I read the newspapers every day, Moroni, and I haven't seen anything yet. Have you?"

"All right. You win. Just tell me one thing. Do I get in to see Pepper or not?"

"My advice to you, Moroni," Howe said, raising his voice, "is to mind your own business."

Two men big enough to have given Goliath a hard time stepped onto the roof and took up positions on either side of the stairway.

"Please escort Mr. Traveler out of the building," Howe told them before turning his back on Traveler to stare out at the city.

11

STATE STREET RUNS PARALLEL to Main, one block to the east. Unlike Main, which is graced by Brigham Young's statue at its apex, State is crowned by the Eagle Gate, a seventy-six-foot span topped by the two-ton copper eagle that once marked the entrance to Brigham Young's private estate.

Traveler passed under the bird on his way to the Semloh Hotel. It, too, was a relic of bygone days, with a facade as sad as the rouged cheeks of an old woman.

According to Martin, the hotel had been christened for its owner, a man named Holmes who liked the mystery of spelling his name backwards.

Rain was falling again by the time Traveler entered the lobby. He dripped across threadbare maroon carpet to a front desk that was made of dark wood, probably walnut, and was as massive as the pillars that held up the hand-painted stucco ceiling. By comparison, the man behind the desk looked puny, though he stood eye-to-eye with Traveler's six feet three inches. The clerk wore a three-piece suit that was shiny by design rather than wear. A plastic tab on his vest said he was Mr. Young. In Utah hundreds bore that name, maybe thousands. Most claimed to be direct descendants of the prophet, whose twenty-six wives had contributed to such a likelihood.

When Traveler leaned against the desk, he could see that Young was standing on a raised platform made of lumber fresh enough to bleed resin around the nail holes. The clerk backed off a step, causing the new planks to creak underfoot.

"They say the guy who built this place was a midget and worked the desk himself," the man said. He wore the lie easily, like an actor. "Now what can I do for you?"

"Have you been on the desk all day?"

Young's eyelids drooped. "I should have known it. You're here about the murder like everybody else."

"I'm a detective," Traveler said, hoping he wouldn't have to qualify himself as self-employed and private.

The clerk pulled at his nose like a man getting ready to do some surreptitious picking. "I've been talking to your cohorts all day. Because of them, business is off."

"Let's start with Rick Dalton. What can you tell me about him?"

"Your people are the ones who came and took him away. So you must know more about him than I do by now."

"Were you on duty when he checked in?"

The man twitched his bony shoulders. "Like I told the others, Mr. Dalton is a regular here. Over the last six months, I've seen him three or four times. I check him in. I check him out. But that's as far as it goes. I don't know anything about his personal life or his business. The fact is, until today he was just another customer demanding fresh towels, soap, or some damn thing."

"What about Zeke Eldredge?" Traveler said.

"He's another kettle of fish altogether. You can't miss him. Has a beard down to here." Using the flat of his hand, the clerk made a chopping motion at the base of his neck.

"He reminds me of those pioneer photos you see of Brigham Young. Of course, Mr. Eldredge is a widower now, because of the murder. Her name was Priscilla, you know, which sounds pioneer to me, too."

"Is he still in the hotel?"

"Checked out right along with the body."

"What about his registration card?"

"Your buddies took it with them."

"The look on your face tells me you remember what's on it."

The clerk sighed. "He left a forwarding address. I remember that because the police are sending his wife's body there when they're through with it. No street address or anything like that. Just Glory, Utah. Wherever that is."

Traveler checked the notes he'd jotted down after his talk with Hap Kilgore. High on the list was Pepper's fiancée. "Would you check your registration for the name Kate Ferguson?"

"I don't have to. Like I told the other cops, we have no record of her."

"I have information that she was sharing a room with Mr. Dalton."

"What our guests do in their rooms is their business, as long as they're not too loud about it."

"Did you ever see another woman with him?"

"One of our bellhops said he saw a lady in the elevator with Mr. Dalton."

"I'd like to talk to him."

Young glanced at the white-faced clock that hung on the wall behind the desk. "I've been on my own time for the past ten minutes. My replacement is late and they don't pay overtime."

Traveler took out a twenty-dollar bill and slid it across the desk. The clerk tucked it into his vest pocket.

"Jimmy's a real baseball buff. He always takes care of

Mr. Dalton when he stays here. But he's off duty right now."

Traveler added a ten. At the twenty-five-dollar-a-day rate he'd quoted Kilgore, he was now in the hole.

"This time of day Jimmy takes a shift as a waiter in our dining room. I'm afraid you'll have to order something to eat if you want to speak with him."

The dining room had the same massive pillars as the lobby. Instead of carpet on the floor there was white tile, the old-fashioned hexagonal kind, small and mosaiclike, held together by grout that had blackened over the years. The one waiter on duty looked old enough to have laid it himself.

When he came to the table, Traveler handed him a business card.

"Sure," he said, holding it at arm's length and squinting. "I remember you. Played linebacker for Los Angeles. My name's Jimmy Vaughn."

The old man held out his hand. Traveler stood up to shake it.

"Would you sign your card for me?"

"Sure." Traveler smiled. People who remembered his football career usually wanted more from him than an autograph.

Jimmy wiped his gnarled hands on his trousers before taking back the card. After admiring the inscription, he blew on the ballpoint ink to make certain it was dry.

"The only time I ever rooted for L.A. was when you played for them." He tucked the card into his wallet. "I never liked them before, or since."

"My playing days are long gone."

"When you get to be my age it'll seem like yesterday, believe me." He shook his head at the menu on the tablecloth in front of Traveler. "I don't think you came here to eat. Otherwise, you wouldn't have given me your card."

"I'm trying to help Pepper Dalton."

"Now there's a man who's had trouble all his life. Do you remember when he played for the Bees?"

Traveler nodded.

"I wasn't a waiter in those days. I had a season ticket. Reserved seats, too. A bunch of us used to sit together on the first base side, behind the Bees dugout. We did our best by Pepper. We cheered everything he did, even foul balls. But nothing helped. He couldn't hit worth a damn. Old Hap Kilgore was the manager then. Why he stuck with Pepper, I don't know."

Jimmy stopped speaking to catch his breath. His eyes, which had lost focus while he spoke of the past, winked at Traveler one after the other. "Of course, I didn't know Mr. Dalton personally in those days."

"What's he like now?"

"He always acts like a gentleman when he comes in here. He overtips me outrageously."

Traveler reached for his wallet.

"No, sir. I won't take money, not from you, not for helping out Mr. Dalton. There's one thing I do want to say, though. If you ask me, a man who was as bad with the bat as he was would never use one as a weapon. He'd probably strike out."

Traveler couldn't help smiling.

"Yes, sir," the old man said suddenly, "the hot beef sandwich is one of our specialties." Under his breath he added, "We've got company."

Traveler glanced up to see Sam Howe's bodyguards crossing the dining room.

"They don't look like missionaries," Jimmy whispered.

Despite their bulk the men might have been mistaken for missionaries on the street, since the church tended to dispatch its proselytizers in pairs. These two even wore the correct LDS uniform: sincere cheap suits, white shirts and ties. But that's where the similarity ended. There was no zeal in their eyes, only danger.

Behind them, dwarfed by their bulk, came the desk clerk. When they reached Traveler's table, the clerk spoke from his position of safety. "Here at the Semloh we reserve the right to refuse service to anyone."

Jimmy backed off a couple of paces, fumbling with his order pad.

Traveler forced himself to stay seated. He slipped his hands beneath the table to hide his adrenaline shakes, the kind he always got before big games. It was his body's way of readying itself for combat on the football field. His eyes would be changing too, turning into crazy linebacker eyes, as his coach called them.

"I'm having dinner," he said. He didn't recognize the sound of his own voice.

"The roast beef, isn't it, sir?" Jimmy said.

Traveler nodded rather than risk hearing the stranger inside him again.

One of the men said, "You're leaving."

"One way or another," his twin added.

Chair legs screeched on the tile as Traveler pushed back from the table. Howe's men immediately eased away from each other so they could come at him from two sides if necessary. Even so, Traveler felt invulnerable, the same kind of feeling he'd had during games, when pain went unnoticed for the moment.

He rose to his feet slowly, being careful to keep the pair in front of him and the waiter at his back.

The desk clerk must have sensed what was about to happen. Words rushed out of his mouth. "You wouldn't want an old man like Jimmy to lose his job, would you?"

"Don't worry about me," Jimmy said.

"We're church security," one of the men said. "We can get uniformed police here to back us up if necessary."

"Am I under arrest?"

"Nothing like that. We're here to jog your memory about minding your own business. That means places like the Semloh are off-limits for the moment."

"Why aren't the uniforms here to tell me that themselves?"

"Because you have friends in high places." Both men smiled, more to show their teeth than anything else.

12

OUTSIDE, THE ON-AGAIN, off-again thunderheads had solidified into a storm front that had brought on an early darkness. Along State Street lights were ablaze, though it was only five in the afternoon.

For a moment Traveler thought of taking shelter from the rain in the Era Antique Shop, which was less than a block from the Semloh. The shop owner kept a pool table in the back for regulars. Although Traveler didn't qualify on that point, he had played a few games of nine-ball while negotiating to have shoplifting charges dropped against Bill and Charlie, both of whom thought of the shop as their own private preserve. When all else failed, they said, donations to the Church of the True Prophet were always to be found at the Era.

Since Traveler didn't know how accounts stood at the moment, he turned in the other direction, jogging up State to First South, where he crossed against the light and continued west toward Main Street. Halfway along the block a covered phone booth, one of the few left in town, looked inviting until he realized two street people had already taken up residence. There was a time when the police had kept Salt Lake's derelicts out of sight on the west side of town.

Traveler shifted gears, moving up to a run. But it was wasted effort. He was soaked by the time he reached the Hotel Utah.

Coming directly from the Semloh made the Hotel Utah all the more impressive. Once it had been the finest inn between Denver and the Coast. Even now, closed for religious conversion, its ten stories of white terra-cotta brick were like a beacon in the gloom. In better times the huge beehive on top would have been etched in neon. At the moment, only the penthouse floor was fully lighted. But then it was the traditional residence of church presidents, living prophets whose power descended directly from Joseph Smith.

Traveler bypassed the front entrance to take shelter beneath the overhanging roof that led to the parking garage. The place looked deserted, an impression that lasted only a few seconds before security men appeared out of nowhere to surround him.

"I'd like to see Willis Tanner," he said, noticing for the first time that remote TV cameras had been tracking him.

The only answer he got was grim looks and the glimpse of an Uzi. Officially, the hotel was still closed for remodeling.

"I'm a friend of his," Traveler clarified. "Moroni Traveler."

His name prompted scowls of disbelief.

Slowly, so as not to alarm anyone, he took out his wallet and produced a soggy business card.

One of the security men took hold of it by the edges as though fearing contamination. He read at arm's length before stepping into a glass booth that had once housed parking attendants. From there he continued to watch Traveler while using the phone.

Traveler smiled into the nearest camera and made no sudden moves. Church security, especially in the vicinity of the living prophet, surpassed the Secret Service.

The man in the booth nodded once, hung up the phone, and rejoined his companions. "Mr. Tanner will be down in a minute. You're to wait here."

Traveler marked time by studying his surroundings. Even the garage area had been constructed of ornate tile, polished brick and scrollwork cornices, trademarks of the French-Classical style that had been in vogue when the church built the hotel in 1911. In those days Mormon leaders were pragmatists. They knew hotels needed guests, and since guests were mostly out-of-state Gentiles who drank, a bar was installed. But as church fortunes increased, pragmatism gave way to zeal. Liquor was banned, forcing Gentiles to flee to Holiday Inns, Marriotts, and Sheratons. Their loss became the excuse to turn the Hotel Utah into another LDS office building.

The side door opened and Willis Tanner appeared. As soon as he saw Traveler he grinned and ran a freckled hand through his red crew cut. "It's all right. I know him. His name really is Moroni, though you wouldn't know it to look at him. The fact is, Mo, you look half drowned."

The security men faded back into their hiding places, but the cameras continued their programmed search.

"Aren't you going to invite me inside?" Traveler asked.

"You're not supposed to know I'm here."

"You shouldn't have told me, then."

Tanner's eyes rolled, more or less in the direction of one of the cameras. Quite deliberately, Traveler stared down at his feet, which were standing in a puddle of his own making.

"I can see that you're cold and wet, Mo. But I've got my orders. No Gentiles inside during the remodeling."

"For Christ's sake. We've known each other since junior high school."

"Exactly. And you still take the Lord's name in vain."

"I take it there are microphones here too, not just cameras."

"Why would you say something like that?" Tanner said.

"I need your help, Willis."

"Officially?" His eyes started toward a camera before he caught himself. The effort triggered a squint. It had been a sign of stress with him since childhood, a remnant of uncorrected astigmatism.

Traveler said, "Do you remember the time my father took us to see the Bees for my birthday? At Derks Field."

Tanner sighed with what sounded like relief. His squint eased somewhat.

"Pepper Dalton hit the winning home run," Traveler added. "The only one he ever hit in his life."

"That was a long time ago."

"Do you remember or not?"

"Sure. So what?"

"Pepper's in trouble."

"Like I said before, Mo, so what?"

"He's in jail on suspicion of murder."

Tanner held out his hands as if to separate himself from Traveler. Squinting puckered half his face. "That's a civil matter."

"He was your favorite player, too."

"I'm too old to play games." With that, Tanner turned and pushed through the side door.

Traveler might have been tempted to follow if the security men hadn't reappeared. He shook his head at them, a signal of truce, not surrender, and then sprinted back to the Chester Building.

A crowd was there ahead of him: Bill, once again wearing his sandwich board, and Charlie, plus half a dozen West Temple winos dressed in dilapidated clothes that smelled vaguely like wet fur.

One of the derelicts, the only one not huddled around the cigar stand's eternal flame, thrust a plastic cup of hot coffee into Traveler's hand the moment he cleared the revolving door.

"Compliments of the house," the man said.

Barney Chester waved from behind the counter, where he was dispensing cheer. When Traveler raised his cup in response, the wine fumes became noticeable. Judging by the smell, Barney had upgraded from jug wine. Traveler sipped, confirmed the assessment, then headed for the elevator.

Bill broke free of the crowd to intercept him in front of the grillwork door. Rain had disintegrated the paper message attached to his sandwich board until only the word TITHING was recognizable.

Nephi Bates retreated into his cage, closing the gate behind him.

Bill pointed at him and said, "There can only be one true prophet. And I am he."

"'Beware of false prophets, who come to you in sheep's clothing, but inwardly they are ravening wolves,'" Bates fired back.

As one, the winos, led by Charlie Redwine, left the flame to cluster around the elevator.

Traveler took a deep breath. The smell of wine was overpowering. "Open up, Nephi. I don't feel like walking up three flights."

Nephi shook his head.

"Dammit." Traveler rattled the grillwork.

Next to him, Charlie began blowing his used, wine-soaked breath into the elevator. The winos mimicked him. Immediately, Bates retreated to the back of the cage, his face pinched by the sinful air he was being forced to breathe.

"Rejoice," Bill said. "This isn't your everyday transgression."

"What the hell are you talking about?" Traveler asked.

Bill held his cup aloft. "No more Ripple, Moroni. No more Thunderbird. That's our motto from now on."

"No more Ripple," the winos chorused.

Traveler pulled at the collar of his wet shirt.

"It's a new city ordinance," Bill said. "Cheap wines have been removed from all downtown liquor stores. The city fathers are trying to rid themselves of undesirables like us. Simple people who want only to warm themselves with drink."

"So what are you drinking?" Traveler asked.

"French claret, thanks to Barney."

Nephi Bates lunged against the elevator door, his hands grasping the grillwork so hard his knuckles went white. The look on his face reminded Traveler of a prisoner doing hard time. "I remember the good old days." His voice trembled. "Before civil rights ruined this country. When police ran people like you out of town. If you tried to come back, they'd break your legs."

"Give me Thunderbird or give me death," Charlie said.

"Thunderbird," one wino picked up, then another. They shook their fists at Nephi.

"I think you'd better take me up," Traveler said to the elevator operator.

The look on Nephi's face was one of relief, maybe even appreciation, as he rushed to open the door. The moment Traveler stepped inside, Nephi slammed the gate shut and rammed home the start lever. The elevator mechanism bucked once before taking hold.

When they stopped at the third floor, Nephi made no move to let Traveler out. Instead, he folded his arms across his narrow chest and glared. His look of gratitude, if that was what it had been, had given way to scorn.

"'And many false prophets shall arise, and shall deceive many,'" he said.

Traveler slid open the door himself and stepped out onto the marble hallway. "If all men were like Moroni," he dredged from long-ago Sunday school, "'the very powers of hell would have been shaken forever.'"

13

THE OFFICE WAS EMPTY and dark, with no sign of Martin's having returned. Traveler switched on the overhead light, which consisted of a pair of fluorescent tubes that blinked but didn't catch hold. He worked the switch again but the flickering continued.

Since the ceilings in the Chester Building were ten feet high, he dragged a chair out from behind his desk and stood on it, fiddling with the murky cylinders until they finally lit up. Even then, they failed to dispel the storm's gloomy half-light. Or maybe it was Traveler's mood, which didn't improve when he checked the coat rack where he'd hung his Levis and shirt earlier. They were as damp as ever. That meant no change of clothes until he got home.

The thought made him squirm. His sport coat had a long way to go before it would be dry enough to call damp. On top of that, its herringbone tweed smelled more like a sea creature than a sheep.

Traveler stripped it off and used it to mop the chair seat before rolling the chair back behind the desk. When he sat down his shirt and trousers stuck coldly to him.

"If you catch pneumonia," he said, directing the words at Martin's desk, "twenty-five dollars a day won't pay the hospital bills."

In his mind's eye he saw his father nodding agreement.

"You're damn right. Anyone with sense would go home and take a hot bath."

Ignoring the advice, Traveler looked up the area code for Orange, California. Once he had it, he called Information and got the number for Charles Cecil. A woman answered.

"Mrs. Cecil?"

"Yes." Her tone was suspicious.

"I'm looking for the Charles Cecil who used to play center field for the Salt Lake City Bees."

"That would be my husband, all right." Suspicion had given way to caution. "But he can't come to the phone right now."

"I'm a friend of Pepper Dalton's."

"Oh, yes," she said. Warmth came into her voice. "What can I do for you?"

"Pepper's in trouble."

"What kind?"

As soon as Traveler explained she said, "I know my husband would want to help. But I don't understand what it is he could do."

Traveler wasn't exactly sure himself. But Cecil was the only member of the old Bees that both Hap and Pepper had kept in touch with over the years.

"What about you, Mrs. Cecil? Do you know Pepper personally?"

"Certainly. He's been a good friend. Chuck and I owe him a lot. He was the one who got my husband interested in baseball cards."

Traveler was about to ask for an explanation when she added, "That's how my husband makes his living now. He sells and trades baseball cards, things like that. At this moment he's attending a card convention in Baltimore. I'm sure he'd like to hear from you. He's at the Hotel Stratford, room three-oh-three-four."

He cradled the phone and sat staring at it, wondering if he should spend money on another long-distance call. Money he might never get back. At the same time, part of him knew such speculation was a waste of time. He had no choice in the matter. Pepper Dalton was waiting; he had to be paid back for a birthday present Traveler had never forgotten.

He called Baltimore, got no answer from Chuck Cecil's room, and left a message saying he was a friend of Pepper's.

The moment he hung up the phone rang.

"Mo, it's Willis. Have you had your office swept recently?"

Knowing Tanner, the reference involved electronic bugs, not cleanliness.

"I'm calling from a phone booth," Tanner added. "I had to walk blocks to find one I knew was safe."

"You're paranoid, Willis."

"I want to help Pepper."

"Come on over and we'll talk."

"Not there. Someone might see me."

"Jesus Christ. When you say things like that, you make me think Nephi Bates really is a spy."

"There's no need to take the Lord's name in vain."

Traveler clenched his teeth.

"I'll meet you for dinner," Willis said.

"Where?"

"Joe Vincent's."

Traveler swallowed another blasphemy. Vincent's was a bar first, a restaurant second. It was on Second South at the corner of Regent Street, known years ago as Commercial Street because of the prostitution carried on there. Tanner's presence in such a place was akin to heresy.

14

THERE WAS ONLY ONE PLACE to sit in Joe Vincent's, at the bar. Willis Tanner perched there like a bird on a power line, waiting for the inevitable surge of voltage that would kill him.

"Why did you pick this place?" Traveler asked.

Tanner scrunched his shoulders, at the same time readjusting himself on the bar stool until he was facing Traveler. "I've heard you and your father talking about it for years."

"You knew what to expect, then."

Tanner's squint worsened, closing one eye altogether. The other blinked, freeing a tear. Traveler hoped it was only a reaction to the haze of cigarette smoke.

"It doesn't pay to set patterns or go where people expect to find you," Tanner said.

Traveler looked around. Every stool at the long, chest-high bar was filled. Beer drinkers flanked them on either side.

"Mormon spies wouldn't defy the Word of Wisdom," he said.

Tanner leaned forward until his head was only inches away. "Never underestimate church security, Mo."

He was about to say more when the bartender brought their order, prime rib sandwiches. Usually, Traveler had a draft beer with his. Tonight, in deference to Tanner, he'd settled for ginger ale.

Tanner sampled his sandwich and made a face. "It tastes like cigarettes. Everything in here does." He pinched his nostrils between a thumb and forefinger and breathed through his mouth, as if that might lessen his sin. "Now, what do you want from me?"

"Do you remember that day Martin took us to see the Bees on my birthday? The day Pepper Dalton hit the home run?"

"Come on, Mo. You can cut the sales pitch. I already said I wanted to help. I have to be careful about it, that's all."

"How far are you willing to go?"

Tanner pursed his lips so hard deep lines appeared in his face. He relaxed to say, "I've read the police reports. I don't see what good either of us can do."

"Did you read them before or after I called you?"

"So the police department is good enough to send us copies of everything that's going on. What do you expect? This is our town. But if I read all the reports that came across my desk, I wouldn't have time for anything else."

"You would if the likes of Zeke Eldredge was involved."

Tanner's head twitched. He turned the motion into a search for eavesdroppers. "For Pete's sake, Mo. Not so loud."

For him that was strong language. But then Zeke Eldredge was an advocate of polygamy, a practice that was still an embarrassment to Mormons a hundred years after it had been officially banned. Even so, there were still somewhere between thirty and forty thousand polygamists in the state. Both in and out of the church.

Tanner checked again for spies. "If Pepper Dalton is convicted, Eldredge could end up inheriting a considerable amount of property. Do you know what that would mean, Mo? Do you? He'd have a permanent base for that crazy sect of his."

He tapped the side of his nose and nodded. "At this moment Eldredge is calling himself the Shepherd of the Flock of Zion. But we feel that's only a cover. Probably the first step toward declaring himself a prophet. Why else would he dress the way he does and wear that long beard? He's trying to mimic Brigham Young."

"Hold it right there. Are you trying to tell me that the church has a vested interest in helping Pepper Dalton?"

"I won't lie to you. It would be much better for everyone if Zeke Eldredge killed that woman. His conviction would give us the opening we've been waiting for. We could drive his followers out of the state once and for all."

His squint dissolved, leaving him wide-eyed with sincerity. "But you've got to understand me. As much as we might like that, we can't afford to be involved, not officially. You know what the media're like when there are polygamists involved." Traveler caught something in Tanner's eyes. What might have been a flash of arrogance.

"You didn't come here on your own, did you, Willis? This spy routine of yours is all part of an act."

"Hey, Mo." Tanner spread his hands against the accusation. "You know me. We've been friends for years."

"That's the trouble."

"I give you my word."

"I'd rather have money."

Tanner drew back slightly. "I seem to remember you saying you wouldn't work for the church again, no matter what."

"Are you asking me to?"

"Maybe."

"Dammit, Willis. What do you know that I don't?"

"I . . ." Tanner smiled wistfully. "How long have we known each other now? Thirty years?"

"Thereabouts."

"These days marriages don't last that long."

Traveler chewed on a bite of prime rib and waited.

"I envy you, Mo," Tanner went on. "I guess I always have."

"You're changing the subject."

"Your relationship with Martin was what I admired most as a kid. Seeing you two together always reminded me that my own father was always too busy to take me to ball games. His duties as a bishop didn't leave him time for things like that."

Traveler shifted uneasily. There was no sign of arrogance in his friend's eyes now, nothing easily readable.

"That day at Derks Field was as much mine as yours, Mo. So is Pepper Dalton. I thank God that I can help him and the church at the same time."

Traveler didn't like the implications of that. But there was nothing he could do about it, not if he wanted Tanner's cooperation.

"Let's start with Deseret Coal and Gas," he said. "What can you tell me about them?"

"There's alien money there. That's the word I get anyway. Investors from California who intend to strip-mine the town of Glory if they can get their hands on it."

"That would certainly put an end to your worries about the Flock of Zion."

"Maybe so, but it's beautiful country, too. Part of our legacy. I . . . we'd hate to see it ruined."

When Tanner used *we*, Traveler worried. There was always the chance he could be speaking for Elton Woolley, president of the church, the living prophet of Mormonism.

Through him came the word of God, by revelation, as it had with Joseph Smith in the beginning.

"On the other hand," Tanner continued, "I hear strip-mining is the only practical way to get at the coal field there."

"Let's back up a bit. Are you telling me that the church has no investment in Deseret Coal and Gas?"

"You hit me with this cold, Mo. I'm not an encyclopedia. I don't walk around with all the answers on the tip of my tongue. All I know is that the company was formed in Park City in the late nineteenth century. At that time it was known as Deseret Mining. Silver was king then. When it ran out, Park City became a ghost town. It stayed that way until developers turned it into a ski resort. That's when Deseret Mining sold its holdings there and moved its office out of the Wasatch Mountains and down here into town. I'm told they have the top floor of the Guthrie Building, under the name of Deseret Coal and Gas."

"That doesn't answer my question."

"California money, Mo. What more can I say?"

"There are a lot of Mormons in California."

"This is the place. Brigham Young said so himself."

Traveler caught the bartender's eye and ordered a beer. He drank half of it before speaking again. "How much money have they offered for Glory?"

Instead of answering, Tanner squinted at his friend's glass.

"I need to know what's at stake here," Traveler said.

Tanner wet his lips. "On the phone you asked about Pepper Dalton. You didn't say anything about Deseret Coal and Gas."

"That's why it's starting to worry me that you know so much."

"Okay, so I may have picked up something from the computer. Five million comes to mind, though I couldn't swear to it. Plus a percentage of future profits."

"Nothing else?"

One corner of Tanner's mouth turned up, the same sly expression he used to get as a teenager, the kind that invariably led to trouble. Like the time he'd insisted on experimenting with the contents of Martin's liquor cabinet, leaving Traveler behind to explain the empty bottles.

His crooked smile intensified. "I did come up with something else. It seems that Zeke Eldredge was a geologist before he founded the Flock of Zion. A geologist would know how much a place like Glory is worth."

"Just as you do, I'm sure."

"Now, Mo."

Traveler closed his eyes and concentrated on chewing a mouthful of prime rib, now cold. Finally he swallowed and said, "For the sake of argument, let's imagine that we succeed in having Zeke Eldredge charged with murder."

Tanner's head bobbed rhythmically like one of those toy birds attached to the rim of a glass.

"Once we do that, Willis, you're in trouble again. The national media will pounce on the story."

Tanner's head jerked to a stop. One side of his face crumpled under the onslaught of his nervous squint. "You're right, of course. We want to eat our cake and have it, too. That's where you come in. You can act as a buffer. In any case, we can probably get by with the status quo, since we've already got Sam Howe to defend Pepper."

Traveler slapped his hands together in triumph. For once he'd maneuvered his friend into a clear-cut admission of church involvement.

One-handed, Tanner began massaging the squint side of his face. "Okay, Mo. You got me. But Sam Howe happened before I got involved. Someone higher up the line hired him."

Since Tanner was in charge of public relations, with unrestricted access to the prophet, higher up meant very high indeed. Perhaps even as lofty as one of the apostles.

After digesting that thought, Traveler pushed away the prime rib and worked on his beer. He didn't speak until he'd finished it. "When the shit hits the fan, Willis, am I going to be able to count on you or not?"

Tanner clenched his teeth so hard veins bulged in his neck. His lips, parted in a grimace, barely moved when he spoke. "It might be best if I took a leave of absence from my job."

Traveler stared. When none of Tanner's usual guile showed itself, Traveler touched his friend on the shoulder. "You stay where you are. Something important might come across your desk. If it does, get in touch with me."

Tanner opened his mouth to say something. All that came out was the tip of his tongue.

"In the meantime, I need some strings pulled to get me into the jail to see Pepper."

"I'll do what I can."

"I don't know about you, Willis, but I need another beer."

Tanner smiled, without prejudice. "Do you remember what we drank at that ball game?"

"Soda pop, I think."

"Coke, Mo. A deadly sin."

Traveler closed his eyes. He recalled hot dogs, peanuts, ice cream bars, and soda pop. Generic soda pop.

"You've got a better memory than I do," he said.

"Breaking the Word of Wisdom the first time isn't easily forgotten."

Other transgressions hadn't been long in coming, Traveler remembered. After their foray into the liquor cabinet, the two of them had been caught sneaking cigarettes.

"Come on," Tanner said. "I've breathed in enough sin for one night. Let's get out of here."

Once beyond the glow of Joe Vincent's, the night sky asserted itself, showing off its stars. To the west, lightning was striking Antelope Island in the middle of the Great Salt Lake.

Traveler and Tanner headed that way, toward Main Street, walking side by side, close together but without touching. A cool mountain breeze was at their backs. Traveler hunched his shoulders, thankful that he'd taken the time to go home and change clothes before meeting his friend.

Tanner drew a deep, noisy breath, then let it go with a sigh. "Do you smell that? You can taste the Wasatch tonight."

Traveler filled his lungs. "I've always thought Salt Lake had a smell all its own."

Tanner pounded Traveler on the back. "You're learning, Mo, what Brigham Young knew the first time he set eyes on this place. That this is the promised land. The land of Zion. It belongs to us and to our children. That has to come before anything else."

At that moment Tanner sounded exactly like his father, Willis Sr., who'd cornered Traveler at every opportunity to proselytize from *The Book of Mormon*.

"You understand what I'm saying, don't you?" Tanner continued. "Never put me in a position where I have to choose between the church and a friend."

"Are you reneging on your offer of help already?"

"I just want everything put into perspective, Moroni. I don't want any misunderstanding between us."

15

THE NIGHT-LIGHTS were on at the temple grounds when Traveler picked up his car from the lot down the block. The temple's six gray granite spires stood out like spears thrusting against the night. Atop the tallest one, the golden statue of Moroni glistened, his trumpet poised to call the dead.

Traveler listened. The sound of thunder, muted against the wind, came to him from the west. When he looked in that direction, lightning from the storm had grown so distant it was no more than a flicker on the horizon.

He drove east on South Temple. Estates had lined that street all the way up to the foothills when he was a boy. Now many of them were converted law offices and mortuaries.

At Virginia Street he turned left, then left again on First Avenue. The Traveler family home, a single-story adobe with green shutters and a picket fence, was one of the oldest in town. It had been built within a decade of Brigham Young's arrival in 1847. Its thick walls, meant to withstand Indian attacks, kept the place cool on the hottest days. At the moment a man was standing under the porch light, cranking the old-fashioned doorbell.

Traveler pulled into the driveway and parked behind his

father's station wagon. As soon as he got out of the car he noticed that the man was wearing a gray suit and tie, the uniform of civil servants and missionaries. Only missionaries proselytized in pairs.

At Traveler's approach, the man held a hand to his forehead to shield his eyes from the overhead light. Judging by his anxious squint, he couldn't penetrate the darkness.

Traveler halted just beyond the edge of light. "What can I do for you?"

"I'm here on official business," the man said, his voice loud enough to be heard next door.

Traveler said nothing. As the silence grew the man began to squirm, a motion emphasizing the fit of his suit. Its sleeves reached his knuckles. Its trousers bagged at the knees while scraping the ground behind his heels at the same time.

"What kind of business?" Traveler said.

"Process server."

Traveler stepped into the light. At the sight of him, the man's eyes widened. His head jerked from side to side as he sought lines of retreat. His hands came up as if to ward off a blow. "I'm just doing my job, mister."

Traveler let him off the hook. "Relax. I've served them myself."

"Shit. One look at you and I thought I was a goner. What do you weigh, two-fifty?"

"I did once."

The man banged himself on the forehead with the heel of his hand. "Christ, what a dummy I am. Moroni Traveler. I should have remembered. You used to play linebacker for L.A., didn't you?"

"I was young then."

"This is for you, then." Gingerly, he reached into his pocket to retrieve a subpoena.

Traveler read the name typed on it and shook his head. "This says Moroni Traveler, Sr. I'm junior. Senior is five-six and weighs one-forty." When he tried to return the subpoena, the man backed off.

Traveler took out his wallet and displayed his driver's license.

"That doesn't mean shit to me. The name I got was Moroni Traveler. That's you. There can't be more than one of you named for an angel, not at this address."

With that, the man feinted one way and ran the other. Traveler let him get away.

Martin opened the door so quickly he must have been waiting on the other side. "You shouldn't have accepted it." He grabbed hold of Traveler's arm and tugged him inside. "And don't go spreading lies about me either. I'm short enough as it is. So don't tell people I'm five-six when I'm five-seven."

Traveler stared at his father, who'd gone up on tiptoe as if to prove his point. "There's no sense fighting it, Dad. They're going to serve you sooner or later."

"Not me. I'm prepared to hide out for as long as need be."

"People have tried that on us before."

"That's right. I know all the tricks. I know something else, too. A friend of mine down at the courthouse tipped me off about this. He said this was one subpoena we didn't want."

"We? I didn't see my name on it."

"What the hell. The damage is done." Martin snatched the subpoena and tossed it onto the mantel, knocking over several family photographs, including his and Kary's wedding picture. When he saw what he'd one, he smiled at his son. "Too bad women aren't what they appear to be."

"I know better than to ask what that means."

"I've taught you something, then."

Traveler sagged into one of two tilt-back recliners that flanked the fireplace. Companionably Martin took the other one, kicking back until he was staring up at the low pioneer ceiling. Around its border was a scrollwork molding too elaborate for the size of the room.

"Your dear departed mother would have hated to see us like this," Martin said.

Traveler sighed quietly. It was always *your* mother, never *my* wife.

"I can hear her now. 'What have you two men done to my living room?' *Men* she always pronounced like some sort of subhuman species."

A groan came from the springs in Martin's recliner as he twisted around to view the antique pool table he'd recently installed in the living room. Its addition left little space for anything else.

"'Look at this place,' she'd say. 'It's no better than one of those West Temple bars you like so much. Where women aren't welcome.' To that, I say fine. Let's you and I play a game of pool right now, eh, Mo?"

"We already have a game in progress, if I'm not mistaken. And so far, I'm losing."

Martin snorted. "What would you say to her, Moroni? If she came back to us here and now."

Traveler knew better than to reply. Rambling on about Kary was his father's way of working himself up to something.

"Do you remember the chairs your mother had in here?" Martin slapped the leather arm of his recliner. "A pair of fussy Victorian pews with carved backs and needlepoint seats. She hired a decorator to pick them out. If sitting on them was any proof, they must have been designed as instruments of torture. Not that she ever allowed us to sit on them, of course."

The chairs in question, carefully covered by plastic sheets, had been moved to his father's bedroom. Every so often he threatened to hold a garage sale and auction them off to the highest bidder.

"She said they were heirlooms," Traveler said.

Martin kicked off one shoe, then the other. "I used to drive her crazy doing this. Making myself comfortable."

With an exaggerated gesture he cupped a hand to one ear. "I can hear her nagging right now. 'Don't start shedding your clothes, Martin. Stay decent in case company drops by.'"

Traveler smiled. His mother had said the same thing to him often enough, using the prospect of "company" like someone else would the bogeyman.

"Decent. That was a word your mother loved. Everything had to appear decent. What was going on underneath made no difference to her, so long as company could drop by and be satisfied."

His father chuckled. "Your Claire is another kettle of fish altogether. Appearance of propriety is not her strong suit."

"Meaning?"

"You'd better read the subpoena."

Traveler righted himself and retrieved the document from the mantelpiece. While standing there, he organized the family photographs into their proper order again, a chronological progression from left to right beginning with his grandparents. Traveler resembled none of them except the dentist, Ned Payson, who came from his mother's side of the family and was, according to Martin, a harbinger of Kary's personality.

He read the subpoena standing up, his back to the hearth. Moroni Traveler, Sr., was named in a paternity suit. He was, according to plaintiff, Claire Bennion, the father of her unborn child.

"When I saw her the last time," Traveler said, "there was no baby and no sign of one."

"How long ago was that?"

"Christ, I don't know." Traveler counted on his fingers. "Six months at least."

"It takes nine."

Traveler counted in his mind. "I haven't slept with her in over a year."

"If you don't touch anymore, why do you bother seeing her?"

"That's a good question. I know better, but just can't help myself. It's like being addicted to drugs. I . . . shit, I don't know."

"You don't have to explain, not to me. Like father, like son says it all. Once your mother got her hooks into me, she wouldn't let go either. And I didn't have the gumption to wiggle loose."

"You loved her, though. I know it."

"Do you? What about Claire? Do you love her?"

"Wait a minute. You're the one who's named in the paternity suit. Maybe I should be jealous." Traveler tried to hold a straight face but couldn't.

"You can make fun all you want, but it makes a man my age feel proud." Martin rubbed his hands together. "And you thought I was past it."

Living with Claire had made Traveler feel past it after a few weeks. But that was only one of the reasons he'd moved out, leaving his apartment to her and coming home to live with his father.

"She must be crazy," Traveler said.

"I told you that the first time you introduced me. But then I had the advantage of having known your mother at Claire's age."

Traveler had no recollection of such a comment. But he wouldn't have listened anyway, not then, not when Claire had him mesmerized with those eyes of hers. Eyes that burned with promises of sensuality.

"She can't expect to win in court," Traveler said. "You've never been alone with her, for God's sake."

Martin raised an eyebrow. "I told you I had a lady friend."

"Don't give me that."

"Don't you think I can get it up anymore?"

"That's not the point. You said yourself that Claire and Kary were just alike."

"That's the curse of being human," Martin said. "We never learn from past mistakes." He scratched his head. "I wonder if she'd settle for a proposal of marriage?"

16

CLAIRE WAS ONE OF THOSE people who change apartments as often as they do friends, every few months. The only place she'd hung on to longer was the apartment Traveler had abandoned to her. As far as he knew at the moment, her latest habitat was the Norma Jean Arms on West Baltic Court, the wrong side of town but still within walking distance of the temple.

The three-story building, aglow with security lights set into roof and ground alike, was built of dark glazed brick the color of old slate. Wide, overhanging eaves dominated the roofline and cast deep shadows into a small central courtyard. Directly above that courtyard, exterior stairs as graceless as metal fire ladders clung to the facade.

Next to the front door, a small slab of granite bore the chiseled date 1917, as if the Norma Jean Arms were a monument to a war architect who learned his trade building barracks. The tenant directory, a row of rusty metal slots into which paper tabs could be fitted, made no mention of Claire Bennion.

Traveler rang the manager's bell. Half a minute later hall lights as bright as floods snapped on.

The woman who came to stare at him through the heavy glass door wore a black dress that covered her from ankle to jaw. Her silver-gray hair had been braided and then wound into a bun at the back of her head. Looking at her, Traveler was reminded of history book pictures of early Pennsylvania Quakers.

Carefully, she fitted gold-rimmed glasses to her eyes, which widened once they had him in proper focus. Her colorless lips pressed together in disapproval.

"I'm here to see Claire Bennion," he said.

She shook her head.

"Claire Bennion," he said, raising his voice.

Her head kept shaking, either a denial of Claire's presence or the woman's inability to hear him through the door.

Smiling with what he hoped was reassurance, Traveler pressed his wallet against the glass to display his state investigator's license. Her lips moved slightly as she read the fine print.

"It's important," he said.

Grudgingly she opened the door but kept the nightchain in place.

"Do you realize the time?" she said. Her voice was as drab as her dress.

"I know it's ten o'clock, ma'am. I'm sorry."

"That woman isn't here anymore."

"Are you saying she's moved?"

"The rent's paid for a month yet, thanks to one of her men friends. But she packed up just the same."

"Do you know her new address?"

The woman smiled suddenly, though with more malice than glee, he thought.

"Maybe you'd better come in and talk to the people living in her apartment." She disengaged the chain. "Three C. I'm the manager here. Mrs. Bothwell. Whatever you do with them is all right with me."

The music coming from 3C could be heard as soon as he set foot on the third floor. By the time he reached the apartment, the sound was loud enough to set his teeth on edge. He pounded on the door.

A moment later the music died off and someone shouted, "Who the fuck is it?"

Traveler slammed both fists against the panel.

"All right, for Christ's sake. I'm coming."

The door opened tentatively. The man standing there—chest expanded, teeth clenched, eyes flashing, brimming with aggression—deflated at the sight of Traveler. His hands fluttered to show they were empty. His naked feet shuffled. "Hey, man, sorry about the noise. We'll keep it down from now on."

"Claire Bennion," Traveler said. "This is her apartment."

The man glanced over his shoulder. Behind him three people were sitting on the bare floor, two women and a man. They had the rumpled, grimy look of squatters. None of them was more than thirty, but they'd already surrendered to middle age.

The room held no furniture, only a few molting pillows and a cut-down coffee can that was being used as an ashtray.

"Invite him in, Davie," one of the women said. "Me and Belle will make him forget Claire."

Davie hunched his shoulders apologetically. "I think he's a cop."

"He's too big for that," she said. "He stands out."

"I'll bet he's big all over," Belle added.

Davie, who'd been watching Traveler closely for reaction, said: "Forget it. Can't you see he's not interested?"

"Only in Claire Bennion," Traveler said.

"Shit, man. We subleased this place from her."

Traveler leaned against the doorjamb and folded his arms. Even from there he could smell stale sweat and the lingering aroma of whatever they'd been smoking. It smelled worse than Charlie Redwine's usual concoctions.

"We've got a paper to prove it," Davie said. "Somewhere." He looked to the others for support. They nodded their heads in agreement.

"Show me," Traveler said.

"You can't expect me to put my hands on it right now. But we paid her good money to stay here."

"How much?"

"All we had. We're supposed to send her more next month."

That sounded like Claire all right, her way of thumbing a nose at people like Mrs. Bothwell.

"Where is she?" Traveler asked.

"How should we know, man?"

"You just said you had to send her money."

Davie spread his hands, a gesture meant to alleviate his lie.

"She told us not to worry about it," Belle helped out. "She said she'd be in touch."

Davie rubbed one foot against the other. "That's right. I remember now. Claire said if we didn't hear from her, someone else would be coming around. That must be you."

Now *that* was vintage Claire, Traveler thought. "She must have left a message, then."

Davie grinned. "Only if you're the Angel Moroni."

"The Moroni part is right."

"We weren't supposed to mail it or anything like that, but only give it to you if you showed up in person."

He snapped his fingers and Belle retrieved a dingy envelope from the nearest windowsill. It had been ripped open and then Scotch-taped shut again.

Inside the envelope was a Chance card from a game of Monopoly. It read: GO DIRECTLY TO JAIL. DO NOT PASS GO, DO NOT COLLECT $200.

17

"IT'S JUST AS WELL you didn't find Claire," Traveler's father said the next morning. He was standing in front of the kitchen stove waiting for the coffee to perk. His maroon pajamas, form-fitted with elastic cuffs at both wrist and ankle, reminded Traveler of long johns. "It's bad luck to see the bride before the wedding."

Traveler spoke through a mouthful of oatmeal, the same lumpy cereal Martin cooked day after day on the assumption that it was good for one and all. "You're the one she subpoenaed. You're the groom."

"You don't believe that any more than I do."

Traveler swallowed without chewing. "Your name was on the document."

"Never believe what you read," Martin said. "Especially when it concerns women."

"That's exactly why I went to her apartment last night. Former apartment, I should say. She left a clue behind for me when she moved out."

"Doesn't she always?"

"If you want to see it for yourself, it's on the mantel next to your wedding picture."

As soon as Martin left the kitchen, Traveler dumped the remains of his oatmeal into the garbage bag under the sink. Had his mother been alive she would have scolded by rote. "Think of all the starving children in China."

These days she'd probably say, "Think of the starving Gentiles on the West Side." The truth of that made Traveler feel guilty, but not enough to eat more of his father's oatmeal.

Martin returned waving the Monopoly card. "You should have rousted me out of bed when you came home last night."

"It was after midnight."

"A detective could wait all his life for a clue like this."

"I went to a bar after I left the apartment."

"You should be ashamed of yourself. I would have gone looking for Boardwalk or Park Place."

"The card says go directly to jail. The best I could come up with was the Lock-Up on South Main."

Martin took his place at the kitchen table, where he pushed his half-eaten bowl of mush to one side and laid the Monopoly card in its place. Top up, the card said only CHANCE.

He turned it over and read out loud. "Go directly to jail. Do not pass Go, do not collect $200." He tapped the card with a fingernail. "If I know women, that's what she wanted you to think. That the Lock-Up Bar and jail are one and the same. But that would be too easy. Trust me. Women's minds don't work that way."

"I thought it was worth a try."

"On the other hand, that's just what she might want us to think, that the obvious was too obvious so we'd ignore it."

"Now I know why I didn't wake you up last night."

"All right. You tell me. Where are you going to start looking next?"

"At State Street and Broadway."

"I don't get it."

"That's where the Saints baseball team has its offices."

18

THIRD SOUTH IS CALLED Broadway for a few blocks in the heart of town. The only trouble is, the great department stores that once helped Broadway live up to its name—the Paris Company, Auerbach's, and Keith O'Brien's—are long gone.

Yet somehow the Brooks Arcade Building had survived, though most of its first-floor shops were boarded up. Romanesque in style, three stories of pie-shaped gray-brown Kyune sandstone, it was originally meant to rise six floors but was cut down to size by the depression of 1893. It was built for a man named Julius Brooks, one of the first Jews to settle in Salt Lake City, the only place where he qualified as a Gentile.

One look inside told Traveler the wrecker's ball couldn't

be far away. The Saints baseball team, he decided, wasn't exactly a thriving business.

He didn't bother looking for an elevator, but settled for the stairs. Halfway to the second floor, the memory hit him, as painful as a sucker-punch. He'd been seven, maybe eight, accompanying his mother to a podiatrist's office on the top floor of the Arcade. Because of midday traffic, she'd been forced to park several blocks away.

"Hold on to my hand," she'd said the moment they got out of the car. "Your father ought to be here to see me through. Since he isn't, you'll have to be the man."

Ingrown nails in both big toes made her walk on her heels. Every so often she'd lose her balance and catch herself on his shoulder. Each time she'd complain, "It's only because of men that women wear foolish shoes and ruin their feet."

The doctor's waiting room had pictures of feet on the wall. An oversized wooden model of a foot, complete with moveable toes, stood on a pedestal near the nurse's window.

Traveler's mother sat him next to a low table covered with magazines he didn't like. "You'll have to be brave and wait out here for me." She smelled of whisky when she kissed him on the lips.

Hours later, or so it seemed to him at the time, she emerged from the inner office. Her toes, bandaged grotesquely, protruded from notches that had been cut into her shoes. Walking her back to the car had embarrassed him immensely.

Traveler pushed through the second-floor door and into an improvised lobby. Chest-high half-walls, papered with Saints banners and photographs, blocked off the corridor in either direction. As a result, only two offices could be accessed from the stairwell. Both had their doors open. The sound of typing came from the one on the left.

He walked over and looked inside. A man about forty, immaculately dressed in a dark suit, his white shirt bright enough to cause snow blindness, was attacking an IBM electric with two fingers. His prematurely gray hair shone like silver. He was, Traveler thought, the kind of man who'd look the same at seventy as he did now.

Traveler knocked on the door frame.

"I'll be with you in a minute," the man said without looking up. "I didn't expect you to get here so quickly. Take a look around if you'd like. There are autographed photos to match the ones on the wall if you're in the market."

Traveler leaned against the frame and waited.

The man glanced up. Instead of the usual appraisal of size or sign of recognition, his face flickered with annoyance. "You might try the next office while you're waiting. We've got Saints caps to spare. You're welcome to take one. The fact is, you'll be doing us a favor. We need all the advertising we can get."

Before Traveler could introduce himself, the man waved him on his way with the comment, "They'll be collector's items one of these days. You can take my word for it."

The adjoining office contained a mound of cardboard boxes stacked head high. At the top of the pile a carton had been torn open. The caps inside were the adjustable kind. One size fits all.

He was fitting one onto his head when the silver-haired man joined him in the crowded office.

"It saves money to order them in bulk," he said, and handed a sealed envelope to Traveler. "How soon will you deliver this?"

Traveler read the typed address: Golly Simpson, care of the Phoebe Clinton Home, 12th East between Eighth and Ninth South.

"Without a stamp on it, your guess is as good as mine."

"You're not the messenger?"

Traveler shook his head.

"I'm sorry. I'm Jessie Gilchrist, managing partner of the Saints." He held out a hand for shaking. "What can I do for you?"

"For one thing, you can tell me about Golly Simpson."

Gilchrist used the hand to take back the envelope. He didn't seem the least bit intimidated by Traveler's bulk. "I don't know who *you* are."

Traveler told him.

"And what do you want with the Saints?"

"I've been asked to help Pepper Dalton."

"I feel sorry for Mr. Dalton. But why does that entitle you to ask questions about Mr. Simpson?"

"I ran into him at Derks Field yesterday. I got the impression he was spying on me."

Gilchrist buried the envelope in the inside pocket of his suit coat before retreating to his office. Once there, he moved behind his desk. Traveler settled into one of two facing chairs.

"I might as well be honest with you," the man said. "I'm putting a deal together to sell the Saints. Simpson's one of my advisers."

Gilchrist opened a desk drawer and brought out a bottle of air freshener. He raised the wick without taking his eyes from Traveler. "Golly's done some scouting for me in the past. High schools, semipros, things like that. He has a great eye for talent. That's why I asked him to prepare a player report for potential buyers. The sooner the better, I say. The cost of running the Saints is eating me alive."

"If Simpson works for you, why send his mail to an old folks home?"

"He's on the road a lot, so I send it to his sister, who works there."

"The road he took yesterday was right behind my car. He followed me."

Gilchrist pulled at his lip. "Maybe he thought you were a scout from some other team."

"Sure he did."

"Believe me or not, Mr. Traveler. It's all the same to me."

Traveler got to his feet and wandered around the office, examining it carefully. Underneath the team banners, T-shirts and caps that had been stapled to the walls, the plaster was disintegrating, the paint crumbling to dust. A century's worth of mold and mildew was thumbing its nose at Gilchrist's deodorant.

Traveler took the cap from his head. It, too, had absorbed the smell of the Brooks Arcade. "As I understand it," he said, "Pepper Dalton has made an offer for the Saints."

"That's correct as far as it goes."

"He has a man at the Phoebe Clinton, too."

"If you mean Hap Kilgore, he's an old man, nothing more."

"He's a friend of mine."

"That doesn't change anything. Neither man figures into the equation any longer, not with Dalton in jail and out of an inheritance."

"And if he's found innocent?"

Gilchrist stood and placed his right hand over his heart. "Look at this place, Mr. Traveler. I can't afford to wait for the trial. If the truth be known, I can't wait until next week. I'm drowning in red ink."

"Do you have other offers?"

"I will soon enough, once the word goes out that I've dropped my price for the Saints. I have no choice, really, not with Dalton out of the picture."

"I was always a fan of the old Bees myself."

Gilchrist dropped his hand and sat down again. "You

disappoint me. I thought you were smarter than that. You've been listening to old men like Hap Kilgore reminisce. There's no going back, Traveler. You should have learned that by now."

"You never saw him play, did you?"

"He never made it. He was a minor leaguer all his life. Just like Salt Lake."

"And Pepper Dalton?"

"He's your client, Mr. Traveler. One of your old Bees, if I'm not mistaken. Why should I know more about him than you do?"

"I haven't seen him since I was a boy."

"It's best left that way. Games are for young men."

"And you?"

"I don't play games, I run them. That's the difference. Take Pepper, now. If it were up to him, he'd still like to play. He's living in the past just like old Kilgore. There's no future in that."

"On the subject of Hap, why was he fired from the Saints yesterday?"

"I hope you're not under the impression that he actually worked for us."

"I realize that he was a volunteer."

"Hospitals need volunteers, not baseball teams."

"When I arrived at Derks Field yesterday, he was wearing a uniform and hitting fungoes. When I left he was out on his ear."

"What can I say? We kept him around for sentimental reasons. A few of our old-time fans got a kick out of seeing him in the bull pen. They're people like you, Traveler, living in the past to avoid the present."

"Bullshit."

Gilchrist grinned. "Okay, so I thought having the old man around would sweeten my deal with Dalton."

"Did my presence have anything to do with Hap getting fired?"

Gilchrist ran a hand over his perfect hair. "I know who you are. I'm a sports fan, too, in addition to being a businessman. But unlike you, I don't quit when things go wrong. You walked away from the Hall of Fame because of an accident. I, on the other hand, would have played all the harder. You see, fear was on your side then. Every time someone tried to run against you, they'd see that guy you crippled. They'd see themselves in a wheelchair for the rest of their lives."

Traveler tossed his Saints cap onto the desk. "Football's a game, just like baseball. It shouldn't be worth a man's life."

"To most athletes their game is their life. Ask Hap if you don't believe me. I killed him yesterday in a manner of speaking. But I didn't have any choice, really. He was Pepper's man, not mine. Once Pepper took himself out of the running by killing that woman, there was no need to keep Hap around."

"He wasn't doing any harm."

"Our insurance people didn't like it. They wouldn't cover us if he got hurt on the field."

"You could have asked him to sign a waiver."

"Give me one good reason why we should want to keep an old fart like Hap around."

"Experience," Traveler replied.

19

THE LOBBY OF THE Chester Building was empty. Even the cigar counter had been deserted, though its eternal flame burned on. Only Nephi Bates was at his post.

He scowled at Traveler, at the same time adjusting earphones that were plugged into a cassette player that hung from a neck strap. As soon as Traveler stepped inside the elevator Bates said, "Floor, please?"

"The same as always."

With a shake of his head Bates cranked up the volume. Then he carefully mouthed, "Floor, please?"

"You win." Traveler held up three fingers. One of them, he noticed, had bluish stain at its tip. No doubt the result of cheap dye from the Saints cap he'd tried on.

Bates slammed the accordion door with one hand and whacked the start lever with the other. The elevator bucked violently. Traveler lost his balance and fell against the grillwork siding.

Grinning, Bates reversed the lever. The cage shimmied. From somewhere above them came the sound of cables clanging together. The resulting vibration produced a resonant hum that set Traveler's teeth on edge. It also drove the glee from Bates's eyes. He hunched his shoulders protectively, dislodging the earphones from his head. The voice of the prophet, Elton Woolley, spilled out: "O how great the goodness of our God, who prepareth a way for our escape from the grasp of this awful monster; yea, that monster, death, and" The connector plug pulled loose as Bates lunged at the emergency button.

Traveler caught his hand in midair. "No need for that. I'll run myself up."

"Don't move us. There might be damage to the cables."

"Three floors isn't that far to drop."

Bates fumbled for his earphones as if seeking salvation before the fall. He didn't know that Barney Chester had installed a backup safety system on the elevator only last year.

The office of Moroni Traveler & Son was as empty as the lobby. The thought flashed through Traveler's mind that the whole gang had gone out drinking, and then he saw his father's note: "Have gone to Salt Lake International to watch the planes. Will be home for dinner." The airport was one of Martin's favorite haunts, especially when he was feeling down in the dumps or nostalgic. If all else failed to lighten his mood, he'd rent a plane and go flying.

Traveler considered leaving a note of his own. "Am leaving for Fillmore. Won't be home for dinner." But as soon as he picked up the pen, he decided to say good-bye to his father in person. After all, Fillmore was a good three hours away by car. Three hours there and back, plus the time needed to find and interview Pepper Dalton's lady friend and brother-in-law, added up to an overnight stay.

He found Martin at a Sky Lounge window table that overlooked the airport's main runway. Since the restaurant catered to businessmen, not casual passengers, his father had dressed accordingly: gray slacks, blue broadcloth shirt with button-down collar, black loafers, and a dark blue corduroy sport coat. The only jarring note was the maroon neck of his pajamas showing above his collar like a T-shirt.

Traveler sat down, signaled for a menu, and eyed his father closely. "It looks like you had a hard time getting out of bed this morning."

Instead of responding, Martin tapped the window to point out a jetliner that was taxiing away from the boarding area. "I used to love coming out here right after the war. It was better than going to a drive-in movie. You could walk right out to the edge of the runway in those days and see the planes close up. I even brought your mother once."

He shook his head as if to condemn the memory. "In those days there were all kinds of planes to watch. Fighters and bombers. P-38s, P-51s and B-17s. Even B-29s. Now what do you see? Passenger planes lined up like sausages."

Traveler was about to mention the National Guard squadron stationed on the other side of the airport, but then he thought better of it. Martin considered P the proper designation for a fighter plane, not F. He'd said so often enough. P as in pursuit.

"They call this place Salt Lake International, for Christ's sake. Look out there." Martin's finger was at the glass again, this time tracing a line meant to take in the entire expanse of the landscape. "We're in the middle of a desert, land-locked. The only proper name for this place is Salt Lake Provincial Airport."

He paused to grin at his son. "But you know Mormons. They think of California as a foreign country. If they had their way passports would be required. The day that happens, I'll call the place international. Not before."

"It's not that bad," Traveler said.

"Bad! In the old days flying commercially meant something. Traveling by air was first-class, reserved for the cream of society. As for the rest of us peasants, trains and buses were good enough. But nowadays everything's homogenized. There's nothing left to rise to the top except scum."

Traveler sat back. He knew better than to interrupt. That would only prolong Martin's mood.

"Progress is like old age. Inevitable but not worth a good goddamn."

A waitress arrived. Traveler ordered a nine-dollar-and-ninety-five-cent club sandwich like the one Martin already had sitting in front of him. It had been quartered, with the crust removed, leaving four bite-size pieces behind on a leaf of wilted lettuce. Off to one side was an ice cream scooped mound of potato salad.

"Do you remember the old Pilot Café on West Temple?" Martin asked.

Traveler did indeed. The place had been famous for the World War II trainer plane mounted on its roof. "They served chicken in a basket."

"Not quite." Martin tapped his forehead. "Chicken in the Rough, they called it. You know what's there now? No, don't bother to answer. I don't know either. That's the trouble. West Temple is like everything else; it's lost its character. All you see is one fast-food joint after another."

Traveler's memory of the Pilot Café included carhops, which qualified it, to his way of thinking, as the fast-food joint of its era.

A jet landed, a small two-engined commuter, probably from the Coast. Martin watched it all the way into its parking area before continuing. "When you get to be my age, memories from your youth are more real than what happened yesterday. Christ, it seems like yesterday when I brought Kary, your mother, to watch the planes. This place wasn't here then, you understand. The terminal was small and friendly. Not like this concrete monstrosity."

Martin's head tilted to one side. "Listen to me, will you? To hear me talk, you'd think I never learned a thing about your mother. That I just kept on making the same mistakes over and over again."

He sucked in a quick breath as if preparing to go on, but for some reason didn't speak again until Traveler's sandwich arrived, a twin of the one already on the table.

"You know what Kary said to me that day? 'You love these planes because they remind you of the war. That's why you come out here. Because you loved every minute of playing soldier. The killing, too.'"

Sighing, he tilted his head to the other side, and then back again as if listening to echoes from the past. "I think those were her exact words."

"It's been a long time, Dad."

"There are some things you don't forget. Your first woman, even though you may live to regret her. Your first kill." He waved his hands over the table as if swatting at something unseen between them.

Traveler caught his breath, wondering if this was the time when his father would finally end his silence about the war.

Martin snorted, a sound of self-derision. "When it came to men, your mother knew what she was doing. She was no genius, but she was cunning enough. Sometimes I think she knew me too well."

Traveler bit into his sandwich, swallowing a lifetime of questions along with the food.

"'That's the trouble with heroes,' she'd say. 'The rest of their life is a letdown.'"

Traveler looked up to catch Martin watching him. His father glanced away, but not quickly enough. The glistening in his eyes had been impossible to miss.

"Sometimes it seems like someone else fought in my place. At other times . . ." Martin pretended to watch the runway, but the window reflected closed eyes. "Your mother knew how to get at me, all right. But by God she wasn't infallible. Having you for a son is no letdown."

When Traveler reached across the table, his father shook his head and said, "Don't get sentimental on me."

"Dad, I'm on my way to Fillmore."

"For Hap Kilgore?"

"That's right."

Martin plucked at his pajama collar. "That reminds me. I took a collect call for you from Chuck Cecil."

"And?"

"I didn't know what you wanted from him, did I? All he knew was that you'd left your number at his hotel in Baltimore."

"I'm surprised you accepted the call."

"I'm not senile yet. I recognized his name. One of the old Bees, wasn't he?"

"Center fielder."

"That's right. A home run hitter. He says he's attending a convention and that you'll have a hard time reaching him in his room. The best time to try, he said, would be about ten o'clock tonight."

"It was a long shot anyway. He might be needed as a character witness for Pepper Dalton down the line. But that's about all."

Martin forked potato salad into his mouth and chewed on it for a while. Finally, he washed it down with coffee. "What do you think about Cecil as a name?"

The tone of voice alerted Traveler. His father was up to something.

"Come to think of it," Martin went on, "Cecil sounds a bit uppity as a first name. Chuck's probably better."

"Un-hunh."

"Hey, I need your input here. It's not easy being a father. I've been trying out names for your baby brother all day."

"Christ."

"You're right. I should have known better and looked to religion in the first place. Like you, he ought to be named from *The Book of Mormon.*"

Martin's lips pressed together in a tight line, his way of holding in laughter. "What do you say? Mosiah? Jarom? Lehi? Manti? They all sound good, don't they?"

"You might as well make it Moroni the third and be done with it."

Martin spread his hands. "Of course. What a dummy I am."

"Have you been talking to Claire?"

His father sighed so deeply it seemed to deflate him. All sign of mirth departed along with his breath. "The only woman I've heard from today is your mother. My head's full of her memory."

Traveler knew the feeling.

"She wanted more children, you know."

"And you didn't?"

"Someday I'll have to explain our relationship to you."

Kary was inside Traveler's head, too, and always would be. "Haven't you ever wondered about the difference in size between you and your father?" she'd ask every so often, her expression alive with implication. "Your eyes, too. Yours are blue, your father's brown." That was her way, never coming right out with it, but edging just close enough so that he'd known Martin wasn't his real father. "I gave you his name, of course. But that had to be. A woman can't be left alone, not with a new child."

Traveler pushed back from the table and stood up. "If I'm going to Fillmore, I'd better get started."

"Take care," Martin said. "You're the only son I've got."

20

MILLARD FILLMORE IS A forgotten president, except in Utah. There, he's remembered as the first friend the Mormons ever had in the White House. Not only did he sign the bill creating the Territory of Utah, he named Brigham Young its first governor. By contrast, Fillmore's predecessors turned blind eyes to Joseph Smith's murder and the Mormon persecution that followed. Fillmore's successor, Franklin Pierce, tried to remove Brigham from office, only no Gentile had the guts to take the post. The next president, James Buchanan, sent an army into Utah to do the job.

As a result, nearly 6,800 square miles of the state are named Millard County. Its seat is Fillmore, a town of two thousand, some 140 miles south of Salt Lake, on the western edge of the Pavant Mountain Range.

Traveler made the drive in a little under four hours, including one stop for gas. His last trip to Fillmore had been as a Boy Scout.

Except for a fresh coat of paint here and there, the downtown looked unchanged. It still had one main street, with few tributaries. Pickup trucks outnumbered cars. At the moment, most of them were parked in front of the Millard Feed & Seed on one side of the street and the Fillmore Café on the other.

Traveler pulled in beside the town's only theater, the Pavant. The message on its faded marquee looked as if it hadn't been changed in years: FRIDAY AND SATURDAY NITE SHOWS ONLY, 6 AND 8 PM.

Sundays, he knew, belonged to the church, especially in rural counties, where Mormons accounted for eighty percent of the population.

It was dinnertime, with still an hour of daylight left, as he crossed Main Street to the Fillmore Café. A yellow neon sign hung in the front window, splashing its jaundiced heresy of Coors against the glass. When Traveler opened the door, enough cigarette smoke billowed out to account for the other twenty percent of the county.

One look and he knew better than to cross the threshold. It was an all-male crowd inside, honest-to-God cowboys by the looks of them. Shit-kickers who'd consider Traveler's size alone worth fighting about. That and his dude clothes: brown dress slacks and a tan corduroy sport coat.

He smiled—innocuously, he hoped—and closed the door on them. When no one came rushing out after him, he recrossed the road to the Feed & Seed, the only other place open.

The store was empty except for a man behind the counter near the cash register. Faded bib overalls stretched tautly across his broad belly. His smiling face was as round as he was. The lenses of his rimless glasses cut deeply into the flesh around his eager eyes. His short, wiry hair was gray, heading toward white. Yet his face was ageless. He could have been fifty or seventy.

"Emmett Culverwell at your service," he said. He fished a railroad watch from one of two small pockets at chest level on his overalls and checked the time. "I was just about to close up, Mr. . . . ?" From the second pocket he produced a badge which he deftly pinned over his heart.

"As you can see, I'm also the law here in town. I suppose that's why you came to me."

"Do you know me?"

"I've been expecting someone like you."

Traveler tilted his head, a gesture that could mean anything, before turning away to study the Feed & Seed. Its unfinished wooden floor had been grooved by wear over the years, creating hollows in front of seed bins and storage shelves. The spot where Traveler stood, across the counter from an ancient brass cash register, had been worn down to the subflooring.

"You're probably wondering why I'm working the Feed and Seed," Culverwell added, then paused as if waiting for Traveler's comment. When none came he continued. "Ace Hardin, the owner, asked me to fill in this afternoon so he could take one of his quick trips to Las Vegas."

His lips puckered out and made a snicking sound. "Old Ace got that name when our last bishop laid into him for playing cards on Sunday. After that Ace figured he had to live up to the moniker, so he makes dashes across the state border once a month like clockwork."

Traveler had been watching the man's eyes as he spoke. They gave him away. The overalls, the bland deaconlike face, the nondescript glasses were camouflage only. He was as wary as a big-city cop.

Traveler supplied his name and occupation. "I'm doing a background check on a man named Pepper Dalton. I understand he has a house here in Fillmore."

The lips came out again, this time without making a sound. Culverwell massaged them between thumb and forefinger before responding. "He's a relative newcomer in town, you understand. He moved here about five years ago when he inherited the old Tempest place from his grandfather, Curtis Tempest. On his mother's side, that was."

"I'd like to start by talking to some of his friends."

"What are you after, character witnesses?"

"Are you one?" Traveler asked.

"In my job a man has to be nonpartisan."

That struck Traveler as a strange way of declaring neutrality. He said, "I understood that there's a mine involved."

"Not just a mine, son, a whole town, though it's a ghost now. Glory, Utah. Originally built as a company town to service the Glory Mine. Don't judge that place by the name, though. It wasn't church work, not in the beginning. If you know anything about our history, you'll know that Brigham Young didn't want the faithful wasting their time grubbing for riches, not when there was honest work like planting to be done."

"I thought it was a coal mine."

"They were looking for gold, Mr. Traveler. What they found was coal. Some days, when it's particularly clear, you can see the smoke from here. The fact is, Glory caught fire years ago, back at the turn of the century, when a gas pocket exploded. It's been burning ever since. They've tried putting it out several times, but it just keeps on belching fire and brimstone."

"How far is it to Glory?"

Culverwell's face lit up. "You have a long way to go, Mr. Traveler. I can tell that by looking at you. You're a sinner if I ever did see one."

"In miles," Traveler clarified.

The man removed his glasses and began rubbing the bridge of his nose. An outline of the lenses remained behind in the dented skin around his eyes. "As I said, you can see it from here on a good day. But the road into those mountains is a rough one. The last few miles aren't even paved. I've never made the drive in less than four hours in broad daylight. I wouldn't even attempt it at night."

"You said something about a house—the Tempest place, you called it."

Culverwell replaced his glasses carefully, looping the metal end pieces around one ear at a time. "It's past closing time. If I stick around here someone's sure to come in and want to buy something. Why don't we go across the street to the café for a drink?"

Traveler stared intently, seeking signs of motive. He would have bet money that Emmett Culverwell, retirement age by big-city standards, held at least three jobs in Fillmore: lawman, storekeep, and deacon. Maybe even bishop.

"It's either that or the Dairy Queen," Culverwell said, as if sensing that further explanation was required.

Remembering the crowd of cowboys, Traveler said, "I could go for a milk shake."

"Come on. Pepper used to hang out at the Fillmore this time of night. Everybody there will know him a lot better than I do. Besides which, they make a great hamburger."

21

THE NOISY CROWD at the Fillmore Café grew quiet and parted for Emmett Culverwell. Even the cigarette smoke seemed to dissipate around the man as he made a beeline for a window table under the neon Coors sign. At his approach two cowboys, wearing silver belt buckles the size of hubcaps, vacated their chairs.

Two bottles of Coors, without glasses, arrived a moment later. Culverwell held up his, waited for Traveler to do the same, and quoted, "'In my name shall they cast out devils; they shall speak with new tongues; they shall take up serpents; and if they drink any deadly thing it shall not hurt them.'"

Traveler drank. The volume of noise went back to where it had been before.

Winking, Culverwell said, "Never go against the good book," and drained his bottle with an expertise that must have taken years of practice. "Now, son, why don't you tell me exactly why you're here? You see, as the sheriff in this town I've already been informed about Pepper's trouble in Salt Lake. The fact is, I saw it coming a long time ago."

"That's what I like about small-town cops," Traveler said. "They're just like their big-city brothers."

"I'm old enough to be your father, so just tell me where you stand. Otherwise, I put down my drink and run you out of town." He grinned. "Don't think I can't do it, either. Half the men in this place have acted as part-time deputies for me at one time or another."

"There's no reason for me to hide anything," Traveler said. "I've been hired to help Pepper prove his innocence."

"Even if he's guilty?"

"You said you saw it coming. Does that mean you think he did the killing?"

The sheriff's eyes, locked on Traveler's face, narrowed as if searching for a focal point. When he looked away it was to concentrate on peeling the wet label from his beer bottle. "Pepper and his sister used to spend summers here in Fillmore when they were growing up. The Tempests had horses in those days, and Pepper and Priscilla—Cilla, we called her then, Silly Cilla—used to ride up and down the back streets like wild Indians."

Culverwell thrust a hand in the air, spreading two fingers as if signaling a V for victory. It won him two more bottles of Coors. He sucked on one of them for a moment, then leaned back, resting his head against the window. Light from the neon sign yellowed his hair and made him look his age.

"In the end, Cilla turned her back on the church," he said. "That would have been bad enough, but taking up with a man like Zeke Eldredge. The man's not only a heretic and polygamist, he's a maniac. He's been accused of everything from cattle rustling to murder, though nothing's ever been proved against him. But where there's smoke there's fire, I always say."

He turned his head as if to look out the window toward the Pavant Mountains. But Traveler figured all he could see was his own reflection.

"I've been hearing rumors about Zeke for years. Everything from unmarked graves to devil worship. I've been on fishing expeditions into those mountains with state investigators twice now. We never found a damn thing. Once we even had a witness who said that Zeke killed any of his followers who tried to leave the fold. The problem is, cremation would be easy in that mine. It wouldn't leave a trace, either."

The man paused to work on his beer. "I just thank God he stays in Glory and out of my town. As for Pepper, he wasn't a happy man. He wasn't content living with us here. Maybe he thought we weren't good enough for him."

Culverwell leaned away from the window to shake his head. "That's not what I meant to say. It wasn't a matter of goodness with Pepper. It was ambition that drove him. He wanted more out of life than a house in Fillmore and a semipro team to coach. If you ask me, he'd lived too long in the big cities coaching professional baseball. We thought we were lucky to get him when he came here. We should have known better."

He went back to his bottle, nursing it long after it was empty. His eyes, though aimed at Traveler, were focused somewhere else. Finally, he removed the bottle from his lips and sighed. "I went to all our games last year. We got our butts kicked. But then we go up against bigger towns, places like Gunnison, Salina and Scipio, which have more players to choose from, while Pepper was more or less stuck with whoever tried out for the team. The trouble was he still wanted to win. Every time he lost he'd get mad, throwing bats around in the dugout like a maniac. He broke his hand once, punching a six-pack of Gatorade. A couple of times he would have punched the umpires too, if he hadn't been stopped by his own players. That's why I saw it coming, because he got that mad at Cilla when she insisted on living out there in Glory instead of selling it off when they finally got the chance. I heard her say it myself. That Glory ought to be preserved as a monument to Zeke Eldredge's faith."

Two hamburgers arrived, their buns gleaming with grease. Catsup and mustard were already on the table. Culverwell applied both before continuing. "God knows what gets into a woman. Sharing a husband might have been all right in the old days when there weren't enough men to go around. But now?"

The sheriff pressed the lip of the empty beer bottle against his mouth and blew, producing a low, resonant whistle. "Is any of this helping you, son?"

"I need all the information I can get."

"I can't talk when I'm dry or hungry." He took a huge bite from his burger.

Traveler half turned in his chair and pointed two fingers at the bartender, who pointed one finger back at him like a gun.

Culverwell laughed with his mouth full. "Custom has it," he said after a moment's chewing, "that the sheriff drinks free. So Heber there is mad that I've brought a friend along."

"I'm buying," Traveler mouthed at the bartender, while waving a twenty-dollar bill to prove the point.

Heber came running. The sheriff caught hold of the bartender's hand as he was reaching for the money. "This here is Moroni Traveler. He's looking for friends of Pepper Dalton. Or reasonable facsimiles."

Heber used his free hand to snag the twenty. "You know what the word is around town, Sheriff. That Dalton went crazy and killed his own sister."

"Just tell the man who knew him best," Culverwell said, nodding toward the counter, "among those sinners here tonight."

Heber twisted out of the sheriff's grip and sat down at the table. Once he'd snagged a french fry off Traveler's plate he said, "Pepper's team is practicing at the high school tonight, you know that, Sheriff."

"That's right. It slipped my mind."

"Where's the high school?" Traveler asked.

"It's the only field in town with lights," the sheriff said. "I'll take you there later."

Not if he could help it, Traveler thought, but kept it to himself. There was nothing like the presence of a cop, even one in bib overalls, to induce memory loss.

"We've been working on the killing all afternoon," the bartender said. He swallowed the french fry before sliding Traveler's plate his way. "The way we figure it, it has something to do with Zeke Eldredge."

"And what would that be, Heeb?" the sheriff asked before cramming the last of his own hamburger into his mouth.

The bartender plucked another french fry and waved it at the sheriff. "Dalton wanted to sell Glory. Everybody knows that. And why not? I'd do the same thing in his shoes. But his sister was holding him up, standing in line to spread her legs for that bastard, Eldredge. Let me on the jury, Sheriff. That's all I ask. I'll vote for justifiable homicide."

The sheriff washed down his mouthful with beer. "I don't think Mr. Traveler came all the way to Fillmore to find your kind of character witness, Heeb. He wants to help Pepper."

Heber popped the french fry into his mouth before poking himself in the chest. "Hell, Sheriff. I want to help, too. That's why he ought to know about the other stuff, before he hears it from the wrong person."

Culverwell sighed. "All right. Let's have it."

"It's not me talking, you understand. Just some of the guys who remember how close Pepper and his sister used to be." The man cupped the palm of one hand around the forefinger of his other hand. "Too close maybe." He worked the finger back and forth in a crude parody of sexual intercourse.

"You know better than that, Heeb. Kate Ferguson has been Pepper Dalton's girlfriend ever since he moved here."

"She could have been window dressing."

"Look around this place of yours and give me a name," the sheriff said in a voice barely loud enough to hear. What it lacked in volume it made up for in menace, causing the bartender's shoulders to sag. He checked the room and sighed.

"I guess I'm it," he said. "No one else here knows Pepper any better than I do. What else do you want to know, mister?"

Traveler thought that over. "Would you consider yourself a friend of Mr. Dalton's?"

"You mean because of what I just said?"

Traveler nodded.

"We were just talking, that's all. Nobody really believes he was sleeping with Priscilla. Hell, he never saw her often enough for one thing. Nobody else around here did either. We stay away from the likes of Zeke Eldredge."

The sheriff confirmed that with a nod. "People around

here are tired of defending themselves against Mormon-baiters who think we're all a bunch of polygamists like Zeke.''

"You're damned right," the bartender added.

"I'm not here to cause trouble," Traveler said. "Just tell me what kind of guy Pepper is."

The bartender scratched a sideburn. "That's hard to say." He looked to the sheriff for guidance, but Culverwell closed his eyes. "Every time I think of Pepper I think of baseball."

Traveler knew the feeling.

"He used to bring the team in here after practice. After home games, too. The first time they came in in uniform I told them, 'The drinks are on me every time you win.'" The bartender chuckled. "I never did have to pay off, not last season. After losing that last game to Gunnison, I remember Pepper gathering the team around him and saying he wasn't coming back this year if things didn't change. 'You pitchers,' he said, 'I don't want you throwing at batters. I want you hitting them, in the head if you have to. At least once an inning to start with. Let them know we're playing for keeps.' One of the guys said he couldn't do that, not in good conscience. And you know what Pepper said? 'You either play my way or you don't play.'"

22

TRAVELER FOUND HIS OWN WAY to the high school. To get there he had to pass by the old state house, a two-story red sandstone building that looked like a jail. Originally, it had been built as Utah's capitol, since Fillmore was closer to the geographical center of Brigham Young's empire than Salt Lake. Those were the days when Brigham ruled not only present-day Utah but all of Nevada and parts of Colorado and Wyoming.

The chill night air smelled of grass and smoke. Pinging sounds came from the white-hot floodlights where moths were exploding, their remains showering onto the playing field below like dusty snow. The scene had the nostalgic quality of an old movie, one that Traveler had seen but couldn't fully remember.

His arrival brought batting practice to a stop. The players—he counted eight in uniform, one short of a team—began edging toward their makeshift home plate as soon as he neared the backstop. From that distance they all looked young and lean, except for the heavyset catcher.

Once Traveler came within earshot, the catcher raised out of his crouch to say, "We could use another fielder."

The man who'd been batting eyed Traveler silently,

while keeping the Louisville Slugger positioned on his shoulder like a sentry holding a rifle.

"I'm here about Pepper Dalton," Traveler said.

As soon as the catcher heard that, he waved in the pitcher, who signaled to the rest of the players the moment he found out what Traveler wanted.

Once everybody had gathered in front of the backstop, the pitcher said, "I'm Ace Hardin, the acting manager in Pepper's absence."

"I heard you were in Las Vegas," Traveler told him.

Hardin snorted. The lines in his weathered face said he wasn't as young as Traveler had guessed from a distance. "You've been talking to Bishop Culverwell. With him, it's once a sinner, always a sinner."

"He thinks we're all lost souls," the catcher added. "By the way, I'm Fats Cody."

"Emmett Culverwell was speaking as sheriff," Traveler clarified. "Not for the church."

Hardin shifted tobacco from one cheek to the other before spitting disgustedly. "There's no distinction around here. You never know if a sin's going to get you arrested. Or what qualifies as a sin either, for that matter."

The pitcher's comment prompted laughter and a slap on the back from his catcher. Encouraged, Hardin elaborated. "Take tobacco, for instance. Joe Smith and Brigham Young chewed it themselves in the beginning, you know. It was Smith's wife who put a stop to it. She got tired of him and his friends spitting on her floor. So she kept after him until he had a revelation. A word to the wise, so to speak." He nudged his catcher. "The Word of Wisdom, get it?"

The catcher groaned and spit through his mask, though without aid of tobacco.

"What's your connection with Pepper?" Hardin asked before reloading his cheek from a plastic pouch.

"I've been hired by a friend of his to find out what really happened."

"He killed his sister in Salt Lake, not here in staid Fillmore."

Cody jerked off his mask as if in pursuit of a foul ball. "Wait a minute. Before we tell this guy anything, let's see some identification."

Traveler complied.

"What a crock of bullshit," Cody said. "It doesn't take a fancy private eye from the big city to know Pepper wouldn't kill his own sister." With an umpire's gesture, he thumbed Traveler on his way.

"Let's hear the man out," Hardin said.

"He's no private eye," one of the other players said—the first baseman, judging by his oversize glove. "I've seen him on TV."

"Doing what?" Cody wanted to know.

"Playing ball, I think."

"Big league ball?"

"Must have been. Who else would be on TV?"

Hardin glared at Traveler. "Is that right?"

Now was the time to explain about football, Traveler knew, but he let it pass. "I haven't played baseball since college."

Hardin spit again. "I signed with the Dodgers's farm system right out of high school myself. That's where I got the name Ace. They said I always had one up my sleeve because of my curveball." He stuck a finger in his mouth to rearrange his wad. "That was before my arm went bad on me. Now all I've got is a fastball and a knuckler."

Cody removed his catcher's mitt to blow on his hand.

"Okay, so the fastball dies off after a couple of innings." Hardin lobbed tobacco in the general direction of Traveler's shoes. "I love guys your size. You have big strike zones."

"I know I've seen him someplace," the first baseman persisted.

The catcher snapped his fingers. "Goddamn it, I remember now. Moroni Traveler. Named for an angel but played linebacker like the devil himself. He's the guy who crippled that running back. Put him in a wheelchair for the rest of his life."

Hardin grinned so hard tobacco dribbled onto his chin. "I'll tell you what, big man. I've still got an inning left in my arm right now. You stand up there at home plate and hit a few. Then we'll answer your questions."

"And if I strike out?"

"Shit," Cody said. "Nobody hits Ace for the first inning."

"What's the point then?" Traveler asked. But he knew the answer already. They were playing a kid's game, King of the Mountain, with grown-up weapons.

"Are you willing or not?"

Traveler's answer was to head for the improvised batting area they'd been using along the first base line.

"Oh no you don't," Hardin said. "If I'm going to throw my best stuff, I'll do it from the mound." Without waiting for reaction, he sauntered out onto the pitching rubber.

"Choose your weapon," Cody said, pointing to a stack of bats leaning against the backstop. Then he coughed out a laugh and trotted to home plate, where he began taking warm-up pitches.

Traveler removed his sport coat before selecting the longest bat he could find, a thirty-six-inch model that would keep him as far from the plate as possible. But as soon as he stepped into the batter's box he realized the hopelessness of his situation. No wonder they'd been using a makeshift batting area. The pitching mound was in shadow heavy enough to make Hardin look blurred around the edges.

Traveler squinted. It didn't help. By contrast, the area directly around the batter's box was bathed in bright light.

"One more warm-up," Hardin called out.

Traveler didn't pick up the ball coming out of the gloom until an instant before it slammed into Cody's mitt. It was a perfect strike, dead-center in the middle of the plate. He couldn't have hit it with a tennis racket.

He backed out of the batter's box and peered up at the light standard behind home plate. Of the ten floodlights arranged in two rows, half were burned out.

"Shit," Cody said. "Old jelly-leg has got him already."

Catcalls sounded from the outfield, where they were playing Traveler at Little League depth.

"Son of a bitch," Traveler muttered, and stepped into the box. He swung the bat a couple of times to limber up; he willed starch into his legs.

"Hold it," Fats Cody shouted toward the mound. "We've got to be fair." He trotted to the backstop to retrieve a batting helmet, which he handed to Traveler. "We wouldn't want you to get hurt. Not too badly, anyway."

Traveler rested the bat against his legs while he donned the helmet. The plastic headgear amplified the pulse inside his head like the echo of a seashell.

"Ready?" Cody asked.

Traveler tapped the plate with his bat to say that he was.

The first pitch would have made Pepper Dalton proud. Traveler had to throw himself flat to escape being hit in the head.

The echo inside his helmet grew louder as he rose to his feet and dusted himself off. His breathing changed. He stoked himself with oxygen and anger just as he'd done before football games; he ignited his rage.

"Ball one," he said through clenched teeth.

He didn't intend to swing seriously at the next pitch, but only time himself against Hardin's motion. Yet even that was a futile gesture. The man's fastball would have been untouchable in broad daylight for someone who hadn't swung a bat in years.

"Strike one," Cody said.

Strike two seemed even faster. Traveler's swing was no more than a token wave of the bat.

"She-it," Cody said. "We've got an old lady up here."

Traveler didn't get the bat around at all on strike three.

"That's it," the catcher said, coming out of his crouch and removing his mask.

"Hold it," Traveler said. "Ace told me he had an inning in him. That's three outs."

"You're a glutton for punishment." Cody dropped back into his squat and whistled at the pitcher.

This time Traveler was ready for the beanball, dodging out of the way instead of diving into the dirt.

"You've got him now, Ace," Cody called out to the mound. "Let's give him the jelly-leg for real."

Traveler backed out of the batter's box to give himself time to think. Were they being clever? Or were they trying to sucker him? On the other hand, maybe they were underestimating him, figuring that he wouldn't know about Roy Campanella, the old Brooklyn Dodgers catcher. Jelly-leg had been his way of describing the leg-twitching fear generated by a good curveball.

One thing was for sure, if he went into the box looking for a curve, a fastball could take his head off.

"Come on," Cody shouted. "We haven't got all night."

Traveler didn't respond, didn't look at the catcher or the mound. Instead, he grabbed a handful of dirt and concentrated on rubbing the sweat from his bat handle. Ace had said it himself, that he'd lost his chance at the big time when he lost his curve. But there were curves and curves. What might get a pitcher killed in the major leagues would sure as hell be good enough in rural Utah, particularly against an over-the-hill linebacker. Or so they'd think.

Traveler took a deep breath and told himself that it was going to be a curveball. It had to be; it was his only hope.

He stepped back into the box, bending forward at the waist so that his upper body was much closer to the plate than before. If the pitch came up fastball, his health insurance premiums would be going up.

The ball came right at him, waist high. He started his swing certain that it was going to hit him in the ribs. It broke at the last minute, directly into the path of his bat.

He pulled the ball to left field, not much of a hit under normal circumstances. But the fielders were playing in too close.

Traveler sprinted around the bases before they could get the ball back to the catcher.

"I'll be goddamned," Cody said as Traveler stepped on home plate. "That ball broke a good foot and a half. Ace struck out a pinch hitter against Gunnison last week with that same pitch."

Hardin came charging off the mound to say, "Goddamn it. You knew about jelly-leg, didn't you?"

Traveler, who was still catching his breath, only smiled.

"You bastard. There's no way you could have hit me without knowing about it. In the old days, when I was in my prime, I could have told you or anybody else that the curve was on its way ahead of time. It wouldn't have done you any good, not when I still had snap in my arm."

"You promised to answer my questions," Traveler reminded him as the rest of the team gathered around.

Cody nodded. "He's right, Ace. Fair's fair."

"All right," the pitcher said. "What do you want to know?"

Traveler pulled on his sport coat while he thought over how to begin. Finally he said, "What kind of man is Pepper Dalton?"

"That's easy. He's not the kind of man to kill his own sister."

Cody shook his head. "We can do better than that, Ace. Pepper needs our help."

Hardin snorted, then spit for emphasis. "He never struck me as the kind of man who needed help."

"You know what I mean," the catcher said.

"Come on. Use your head. We don't know anything that's going to get him out of jail."

"We could say he was here with us at the time of the murder," the first baseman suggested.

"Hell, yes," Cody agreed. "I'd swear to it."

Traveler gestured for restraint. "I'm sure Pepper would be grateful for such loyalty, but it's not going to help. Right now, I need to get some kind of overall view of him. What he's like personally."

"He didn't like losing, if that's what you mean," Hardin said. "He used to jerk me out of games if I so much as walked a batter."

The catcher shook his head. "Be fair, Ace. You throw half a dozen curveballs and you're in pain. And when you run out of fastballs there's nothing left but the knuckler. When that's wild, you've had it."

"What are you doing, bucking for manager?"

Traveler jumped in before the catcher could think of a comeback. "Just what kind of manager is Pepper?"

"Like I said," Hardin went on, "he doesn't like to lose."

"I've heard that he's an advocate of beanballs."

"So that's what happened. You were ready for me. And I thought I was losing my control."

"He sounds like a violent man," Traveler said.

"Not him," Cody answered. "Not personally."

"What my catcher means is that Pepper told us what *we* had to do to win."

The catcher snorted. "'We' is right. We were the ones

out on the field. When one side starts throwing beanballs, the other side retaliates. Our heads were on the line, not his."

"Pepper's as tough as they come," Hardin said. "He knows the game. The fine points. The strategy. He's better than any of those analysts you hear on television. I've watched him. He plans every move in advance, right from the first inning. Nothing ever catches him by surprise."

Fats Cody nodded his agreement.

Traveler looked at the other team members. "What about it? How do the rest of you feel about him?"

Five minutes later Traveler had a consensus. When it came to baseball, Pepper Dalton knew what he was doing. When it came to people, or players, some liked him, some didn't.

"What about his sister?" Traveler asked. "What was she like?"

Suddenly all eight of them were looking anywhere but at Traveler. When the silence grew uncomfortable Hardin sighed and said, "We've seen her over the years, sure. We grew up with her, for God's sake. But once she took up with the Flock of Zion out there in the hills, we seldom saw her. The fact is, old Zeke Eldredge—he's the one who calls himself the Shepherd—doesn't like letting his women out on their own."

"When was the last time you saw her?" Traveler said.

"That's easy. Two games ago."

"The one and only time she ever came to see us play," Cody added.

"That's bullcrap, Fats, and you know it. She didn't come here to see us. Zeke sent her here to cause a scene." Once the words were out Hardin looked sorry he'd uttered them.

Traveler said, "You'd better tell me what happened."

The pitcher looked around as if seeking moral support. Nobody gave it. "What the hell," he said finally. "Priscilla, God rest her, came right into the dugout and started yelling at Pepper." He indicated the long wooden bench behind first base. "When he tried to quiet her down, she just got louder. She said she intended to shout it to the world."

"Shout what?" Traveler asked.

"That's right," Cody said. "Go ahead and put the rope around Pepper's neck."

"It's no secret. Half the people in town were here," Hardin said.

"Let them do the dirty work, then."

"Don't you think it would be better if I heard it from his teammates?" Traveler said.

"He's right," Hardin said, but didn't elaborate until he got nods of agreement from the others. "She said she'd never sell Glory just so he could play games the rest of his life."

"You might as well tell him all of it," Cody said.

Hardin spit into the pocket of his glove and then began working the moisture into the leather. "Pepper told us—in the strictest confidence, you understand—that he wanted to sell his inheritance to buy a professional baseball team."

"He said he'd give us all tryouts," Cody added.

Hardin shook his head. "I never fooled myself about that."

"You've got five years on the rest of us," Fats said. "You've already had your chance."

"You can't hit me even now," the pitcher responded.

"I've been calling your signals so long I can read your mind."

"You want to try it right now?" Hardin said, gesturing toward home plate.

Before a new king of the mountain could be crowned,

Traveler said, "Is there anything else you can tell me about Pepper?"

"Off the field," Fats said quickly, his eagerness for a change of subject obvious, "no one knew him better than Kate Ferguson."

"They lived together," Hardin added, "though Bishop Culverwell was doing his best to change that."

23

KATE FERGUSON LIVED in a tiny one-and-a-half-story pioneer house at the edge of town. The house was built of quarried stone that looked darkly volcanic. Its architecture, with two windows and one door facing the road, featured wall dormers and cross gables better suited to a mansion. Hundreds of places just like it had been built throughout southern Utah during the last century. Few had survived. Those that did were called, for a reason Traveler didn't understand, the Gothic Revival style.

Kate Ferguson reminded Traveler of a Gothic-looking teacher he'd had in grade school. Both were big-boned and awkward, with salt-and-pepper hair from which pencils protruded. Both wore severe rimless glasses. His teacher's glasses, however, had given her X-ray powers with which to read his errant thoughts.

The Ferguson woman had opened the door with a book

in her hand. She blinked myopically and took off her reading glasses to get a better look at him. Without her spectacles, her Gothic appearance gave way to that soft, gently wrinkled beauty some women achieve in late middle age. Her smile made him jealous of Pepper Dalton.

She said, "If you're Mr. Traveler, I've been expecting you."

He said that he was.

"Fillmore is a small town, Mr. Traveler. Especially when you're already the subject of gossip. I've had several calls about you in the last hour." She hadn't made it clear just who the gossips were after.

"Let me guess," he said. "Was it Sheriff Culverwell who phoned first? Or was he acting as Bishop Culverwell?"

She laughed. "Would that count as one call or two, do you think?"

"There's such a thing as separation of church and state."

"Not in Utah." She widened her smile and beckoned him inside. As he passed close to her, the smell of lemon soap came from the shapeless shirt that hung loosely over faded jeans.

The inside of the house surprised him. Usually the Gothic Revival style squeezed its bedrooms up under the roof where the attic belonged. By so doing, the downstairs ceiling would be too low for a man Traveler's height. But in Kate's house, the upstairs had been torn out, with only the cross-beams left behind. They cleared the top of Traveler's head by an inch, while she had at least a foot to spare. She had added new obstacles, however, a maze of potted plants hanging from the beams by heavy ropes.

The reconstruction had reduced the floor plan to one large room, with a living room/bedroom area on one side and kitchen space on the other. All the surfaces in the house, except the oak plank flooring, had been painted a cheerful white.

She steered him to rattan chairs grouped around a small glass-topped table in the kitchen area. Once they were seated she said, "I know about Pepper's trouble in Salt Lake. A friend of ours, Hap Kilgore, called to let me know. If he hadn't, I'd still be waiting dinner for Pepper. He also said I could trust you."

Despite her wrinkles, Traveler decided she had to be at least fifteen years younger than Pepper Dalton.

"Poor Pepper," she said. "Poor Prissy, too. She didn't have much of a life these last few years, living out in the mountains the way she did. I asked her about it once, why she put up with it. Do you know what she said? That I was the one who wasn't living. That God was with her, not me. What do you think about that, Mr. Traveler?"

"I'm not a theologian."

She stared intently at him before continuing. "People said Prissy and I looked like sisters. I never could see the resemblance, though." She sighed. "Living like a pioneer the way she did, with no modern conveniences, ages a woman fast."

"Can you think of anyone who might have a reason to want her dead?"

"Other than Pepper, you mean?"

"Preferably."

"Pepper's the one you ought to talk to about that. I tried to get through to him myself, but the police weren't very helpful."

"Your fiancé has a lawyer. A man named Howe. He ought to be able to put you in touch."

"I've already spoken with him. Hap gave me the name, but it doesn't mean anything to me. Is he a good lawyer?"

"Sam Howe handles church business. That makes him one of the most important people in Salt Lake."

"I'd better do what he suggests, then."

"And what is that?"

"Don't misunderstand my motives, Mr. Traveler. I love

Pepper and would do anything to help him. But I also know he isn't a killer. In any case, Mr. Howe says it would be a good idea if we got married as soon as possible."

"To keep you from testifying?"

"Nothing was said about that. But that would be all right with me. Unfortunately, I don't know anything worth testifying about. Besides, in a way we're already married."

"What is that supposed to mean?" he said with more force than he'd intended.

"It's hard to explain. You have to know about a man named Zeke Eldredge to understand what's going on out in those mountains I was talking about."

"I know him, by reputation at least."

Her eyes narrowed, causing the wrinkled flesh around them to quiver slightly. "He once pronounced us man and wife, for what that's worth."

"Are you a member of his church?"

"I'm not the kind of woman to share my man. Why Prissy put up with living in a harem, I don't know."

"Then why seek out Zeke Eldredge?"

"I don't see what this has to do with helping Pepper."

"I'm after information, anything that might give me a way to help your fiancé." And Hap, he added to himself. "I need to understand the people involved."

"I see." Kate rose from her rattan chair and ran a finger along a bookshelf that protruded from the stone wall next to the table. After progressing a foot or so she checked her fingertip for dust. "Pepper and his sister own an old coal mine in the Pavant Mountains. And the town that goes with it. A place called Glory. But I'm sure you know this already."

Rather than stop the flow of words, Traveler smiled encouragement to continue.

She did. "For a long time nobody thought Glory was worth anything. Even the Indians wouldn't go near it.

They have legends about it, that it's the home of evil spirits. I guess because of the coal fires underground."

She wrinkled her nose as if she could smell the smoke. "I'm not superstitious, Mr. Traveler. I'm a schoolteacher, an educated woman, but that place gives me the creeps."

Traveler urged her on with a nod.

"You'd have to see it yourself to understand. Anyway, when Prissy took up with Zeke Eldredge, she moved Zeke and his followers into Glory. Pepper didn't raise much of a fuss at the time. But then there was no reason to, since you couldn't give the land away. Of course, Pepper wasn't happy about his only sister taking up with a polygamist. But what could he do? Besides which, a lot of Mormons around here, Mormons in good standing, have more wives than the law allows."

She paused to straighten a pair of scrapbooks that were sandwiched between bookend replicas of the Mormon temple in Salt Lake. "Where was I? Oh, yes. When the offer for the land came, Pepper drove to Glory to try to talk sense into his sister. He took me with him, with instructions to be nice, even to Zeke Eldredge. So when the Shepherd—that's what he calls himself—said he wanted to save our souls by marrying us into his, the one true, church, we went along."

She tilted her head in Traveler's direction. "There are some who would call what we did sacrilege. Are you among them, Mr. Traveler?"

When he failed to respond she closed her eyes momentarily. Her wrinkles smoothed away until her eyes opened and she started speaking again. "You don't have to tell me. I've often been sorry for going along with a man like Eldredge. Besides, you should have seen the gleam in Pepper's eye when Zeke said he was now eligible to take more wives. That it was his duty, in fact. That Joseph Smith had laid down the law in the beginning and there was no getting around it."

She made a scissors motion with her fingers. "I told him what I'd cut off if he tried anything like that."

Her face flushed with color. She touched a hand to her cheek. "You'd think a woman my age wouldn't blush."

She withdrew one of the scrapbooks. "It's Pepper's. Would you like to see it?"

"Very much."

She brought the book to the table and placed it before Traveler. As he turned the pages, newspaper clippings brought Pepper Dalton to life, the Pepper Dalton Traveler remembered from his own boyhood. A tall, lean shortstop, all elbows and knees, who looked damned awkward in photos, but who could field and throw like a big leaguer. According to the clippings, he'd come to the Bees straight out of high school. Fillmore High. Where Traveler had played King of the Mountain less than an hour ago.

"He was my favorite player when I was a boy," Traveler said. "I went to every game I could when he played for the Bees."

"Pepper gets the same look you do when he talks about those days. Past glories and all that. Did you play baseball, Mr. Traveler?"

"Some."

She shuddered suddenly and rubbed her arms as if trying to erase the gooseflesh that had sprouted there. Traveler fought back the urge to help her.

"I told Pepper then and I'll tell you now. I don't believe in living in the past. Using that money to buy a baseball team won't make any of you young again. Not you, not Hap Kilgore, not Pepper either."

"Are you against the sale of Glory?"

"There's a lot of money to be made. All things being equal, I don't mind being rich. But that's not why I'm marrying Pepper."

"Will there be anything left over after he buys the Salt Lake Saints?"

"That's Pepper's dream. A woman should know better than to stand in the way of a man's dream."

"And your dream?"

She smiled. "To get married, in jail if I have to."

Traveler pretended to study the scrapbook. "I understand that Zeke Eldredge accompanied Priscilla to Salt Lake."

"I wouldn't know about that."

"Hap Kilgore said he saw you there, too. In the hotel with Pepper."

"People in this town think Pepper and I live together, Mr. Traveler. But they're wrong. We go to bed together, yes. But he never stays the night. And he won't until we're man and wife. That's my rule."

"You haven't answered my question."

"I was there, yes, on a visit. But I did not spend the night with him in a hotel. The fact is, I never set foot in his room."

"What about his sister's room?"

"I wasn't there either."

"There are witnesses who say otherwise. That a woman was there."

"I'm one of them. Her room was right next to Pepper's. I was in the hall when I saw a woman go in."

"Did you recognize her?"

She shrugged. "She was the maid, I think. She was wearing a white uniform. I didn't pay much attention."

"Could you identify her?"

"Probably."

Traveler thought that over for a moment. Something seemed out of place. Was it her or him? Was she lying or was he asking the wrong questions?

He generalized. "Can you think of anything at all that might help me?"

Her eyes closed. Beneath her eyelids Traveler saw rapid movement, as if she were searching for something only she could see. Finally, she nodded her head. Her eyes re-opened.

"I can't help blaming everything on Zeke Eldredge," she said. "It wouldn't be the first time that man tried to foist one of his women on Pepper. Anything to get a hold on my man, to force him to deed the land over to that so-called church of his. Imagine. Calling themselves the Flock of Zion. Sheep to be shorn, that's what I call them."

She went back to rubbing her arms. "Men can be so foolish when it comes to women. Zeke offered to recruit as many wives as Pepper could handle. Those were his words. Handle! Zeke didn't think I could hear what he was saying, but I did. The old fool."

She wet her lips. "I'm more than enough woman for a man Pepper's age."

Traveler went back to the scrapbook, where Pepper was watching him from a photo.

"What about you, Mr. Traveler? How many wives do you think a man can handle? A man like yourself for instance?"

"My father always said my eyes were bigger than my stomach."

For a moment he thought she was going to ask him to leave. Then suddenly she began to laugh. When she caught her breath she said, "Would you like a piece of homemade pie, Mr. Traveler? What is your first name, by the way."

"Moroni."

"My God, Hap Kilgore has sent me an angel."

"I'm named after my father."

"Who art in heaven," she added, and started laughing again.

"A man shouldn't go to Glory on an empty stomach."

She sobered quickly. "Don't joke about something like that."

"I have to go there. It's my job."

"We all end up in glory soon enough, without going out of our way to find it."

"Pie would be fine," he said.

"A typical man, changing the subject to suit himself."

He started to protest, but she turned her back on him to fetch the pastry. Five minutes later they were eating apple pie with butter melted under the crust. Only then did she resume their talk. "You can't drive to Glory at night. I know the road and I wouldn't try it."

"I'm planning to leave first thing in the morning."

"Do you have someplace to stay?"

For an instant he thought, hoped, that she was inviting him to stay with her.

"I'll call the Paradise Motel and get you a room," she said.

"That's quite a choice, Paradise or Glory."

She ignored the comment and made the reservation. "Paradise in on Main Street," she said as soon as she hung up the phone. "Like everything else in this town."

"I don't think it's as far away as that."

Her cheeks flushed. "You be careful when you talk to Zeke Eldredge. He's crazy."

"How crazy?"

"Just don't look at his women, that's all. And don't take a woman out there with you."

"I was hoping you'd be my guide."

Her head shook, almost a twitch. "I'll give you directions, but you won't catch me up there again. Not ever." She shuddered. "Right after marrying us, Zeke tried to make a trade with Pepper. For me. Two of his wives and a draft choice to be named later was the way he put it, like a baseball trade. Pepper laughed like hell at that. But I was scared right up to the moment we left. I had the feeling that if Pepper had accepted the deal, I would have been a prisoner in that hellhole for the rest of my life."

24

TRAVELER CHECKED OUT of the motel after breakfast and was on the road by nine. He drove north on Interstate 15 to the town of Scipio. There, he topped off the gas tank and checked the water himself before turning southeast on Highway 50 toward the Pavant Mountains.

The sky was clear, the temperature heading into the seventies if the radio was to be believed. But the radio didn't say anything about the thunderheads piling up over the mountains.

About the time he ran out of blue sky, he found the unpaved road that Kate had told him about. He turned off the highway, leaving farming country behind, and began winding his way up onto the Pavant Plateau. The thunderheads looked closer now and more menacing. According to Kate, Glory itself stood at an altitude of 9,000 feet.

He drove cautiously, raising only a small rooster tail of dust. As he gained altitude the clouds darkened. Yet even in such muted light the rocky landscape dazzled him. Outcroppings of red, yellow, and white sandstone reminded him of the Grand Canyon.

By the time the grade changed from steep to moderate, a roadside marker said the altitude was 8,500 feet. Rain looked imminent. Or maybe snow, judging by the way the temperature had been dropping.

When he was twenty miles from the highway on the odometer, Traveler slowed to a crawl. Kate had warned him that the cutoff to Glory was easy to miss. He wouldn't have found it at all if it hadn't been for the old wall she'd mentioned.

When he got out to take a look, the air smelled of ozone and pine. Because of the altitude, jogging the twenty yards to the wall left him panting. He bent over at the waist to catch his breath and read the inscription on the pioneer monument's plaque.

> This wall was erected in 1888 by Mrs. Horace
> (Aunt Libby) Rockwell to shelter the graves
> of her beloved dogs, Jenny Lind, Josephine &
> Bonaparte, and Bishop & Toby Tyler,
> companions in her lonely, childless vigil
> here from 1866 to 1890.

Traveler straightened up and looked around. He saw no sign of a house, nowhere an old woman could have lived. The rutted track that led to Glory curved around a stand of altitude-stunted trees and disappeared from sight. He squinted back the way he'd come. No sign of life that way either. He hadn't seen another car since leaving Highway 50. That was more than an hour ago.

Rain began to fall. By the time he reached his car, the rocky landscape glistened as if it had been polished. For a moment he sat there, staring through the windshield and hesitating. If it kept on raining, the road leading to Glory would turn to mud. Or worse if the rain turned to snow. Even a four-wheel-drive like his Jeep might have trouble getting out of there.

He stepped out of the car again and walked along the ruts to the point where they disappeared behind the trees. From that vantage place the track ran downhill. It also smoothed out after a hundred yards or so, looking compact enough to have been used by heavy vehicles recently.

"What the hell," he said. No sense turning back now that he was already cold and wet. He trudged back to the Jeep.

Ten minutes later he topped a rise. Below him, the landscape changed abruptly. All sign of color ended, replaced by a valley of black soil and rock. The Glory Mine—it could be nothing else—was an isolated reef of coal, an anomaly of nature.

A shroud of dingy fog hovered over the landscape, trapped between earth and sky by the storm clouds. He sensed the town of Glory rather than saw it. It was no more than a flickering smudge of light at the center of the reef. Around it, smoke vented from a maze of underground fissures.

His foot came off the accelerator without conscious thought on his part. The Jeep continued to roll forward, but without gaining momentum because of the wet track.

The flickering beacon disappeared abruptly. His foot, still acting on its own, tapped the brake. He overrode his instinct and drove on by force of will.

As soon as he entered the smoky fog his eyes began to water. The air tasted bitter. The rain on the windshield darkened. He switched the wipers to maximum and leaned forward, straining to keep sight of the narrow trail.

Suddenly flame erupted from a nearby fissure. Then another vented its fire along the same fault line. And another. Like battlefield flares, they lighted the landscape of Glory. He saw weathered buildings, as dilapidated and dreary as purgatory. Charred piles of rubble where houses and barns had collapsed into fire-hollowed chasms. A pioneer cemetery, its crosses and monuments scattered by the angry earth.

The light failed. The road ran out. Traveler stopped the Jeep and exited warily, using his flashlight to check the immediate area for signs of instability. Satisfied that the vehicle was as safe there as anywhere in Glory, he headed for the nearest building. The faded lettering on its clapboard front said: GLORY MINE 1881.

A minor eruption revealed a pair of muddy worn-out minibuses parked nearby. Their rust spots, as encompassing as camouflage, had been splattered with paint as if to prevent further disintegration.

The ground trembled beneath his feet. Steam hissed from the earth, bringing with it a sulfuric stench.

He went back to the Jeep and honked the horn to announce himself. A moment later three men, dressed in yellow slickers and rain hats, emerged from the building.

Violence and murder weren't uncommon among Utah's polygamist cults, Traveler reminded himself. But he left his .45 in the glove compartment just the same, pulled up the collar of his coat, and stepped forward to meet them. The rain on his face felt gritty.

"I'm looking for Zeke Eldredge," he said.

Instead of answering, the trio formed a half circle around him and walked him inside. There, in a large room that housed an open mine shaft the size of a subway tunnel, another three men were waiting. They wore baggy black suits and the full beards that Mormon deacons favored a century ago.

When the first three shed their slickers, more black suits and beards were revealed. Only one man stood out. His head was shaved and so was his face.

"I am the Shepherd," he said. "Nonbelievers know me as Zeke Eldredge."

He was a short, squat man, all muscle, with a nose crooked enough to have been broken several times. His black eyes looked incapable of surprise. He reminded Traveler of a miner or a boxer, anything but a preacher.

"Explain yourself," he said.

Traveler saw no reason to be evasive. He told them who he was and that he was looking into the murder of Pepper Dalton's sister, Priscilla.

"I know you," Eldredge responded. "You represent the devil. Only he would be capable of the sin of fratricide."

"I represent Mr. Dalton," Traveler said, stretching the point.

"The good book tells us, 'Wo unto the murder who deliberately killeth, for he shall die,'" Eldredge said.

He had the cadence and tone of those evangelists who give sharp, dangerous edges to their words. His followers, who'd formed a ring around Traveler, nodded as one. Hatred showed openly on their faces. If it came to a fight, Traveler knew he would have to take out Eldredge first. After that, he might have a chance despite the five-to-one odds.

"And if Pepper didn't kill his sister," Traveler said. "What then?"

Eldredge pointed a finger toward the ground beneath his feet. "I knew, I predicted that they would send someone like you among us. 'The Flock of Zion will be sorely tested,' I told my flock. 'The usurpers in Salt Lake want an end to us, those who hear and abide by the true words of God. They will send the devil's disciple to bring us down.'"

Traveler shivered as a sudden trickle of moisture ran out of his hair and down the back of his neck. The only heat in the large room came from coal burning in a pit that had been scooped in the earthen floor. Smoke from it rose straight up and disappeared through cracks in the warped clapboard siding.

Eldredge's finger rose up to point at Traveler. "Do you deny my revelation?" he demanded.

Traveler said nothing.

Eldredge reached into a baggy coat pocket and brought out a battered copy of a leather-bound book the size of a paperback. A limp paper marker hung down its spine.

"The Book of Mormon." He placed the volume in the palm of his left hand and covered it with his right like someone about to swear an oath. His eyes closed. "I feel the words of God. I see them burning inside my head. 'If ye are not the sheep of the good shepherd, of what fold are ye? Behold, I say unto you, that the devil is your shepherd, and ye are of his fold.'"

From outside came the sound of steam venting from the earth.

"Your master calls," Eldredge said, his dark eyes now fixed on Traveler's face. "He opens the earth to send us a message from hell."

Traveler said, "I was told that Glory caught fire around the turn of the century. That miners hit a gas pocket when they were trying to open up a new shaft."

"The question is, who put that pocket there? God or the devil?"

"I leave that to philosophers like yourself," Traveler answered. "Or should I say geologists?"

"You come forearmed, I see."

"My job is gathering information."

"Here's more for you then. I didn't kill my wife. She was dear to me, as all of them are."

"Even if I grant you that," Traveler said, "there's still the question of background. Would a geologist bury himself in a mine for theological reasons?"

Eldredge spread his arms and pivoted until he was facing the mine shaft. "Hear me, Lord," he said, his voice rising, "who is better qualified than a geologist to fight the devil in this place?"

His words echoed down the shaft. Once they'd subsided, Traveler thought he heard something else. Like the soft murmur of a prayer.

"I can't do my job unless I know more about Priscilla Dalton," Traveler said.

"Her name was Eldredge, not Dalton." Eldredge ran a hand over the top of his head and along his jawline. "I'm in mourning. You can see that for yourself. I have shorn myself, stripped away that which makes me a member of the flock. Only when my hair and beard grow back will God again be able to recognize me."

"Did your wife have any enemies?"

"We all have one enemy. He who waits for us in the pit." Eldredge gestured toward the tunnel mouth. "He's waiting there now, to rob us of our souls."

"Do you know anyone of flesh and blood who'd want to kill her?" Traveler amended.

The man laughed, a short barklike sound that echoed hollowly. "I'm no fool. I know what it looks like to outsiders. Only two stand to gain by her death. Myself and Pepper Dalton. We both want Glory. Me for God's uses, he for money."

His hands squeezed *The Book of Mormon* until they and it shook. Then he used the marker to open the book and find his place. " 'Before ye seek for riches, seek ye the kingdom of God.' Dalton stands convicted by God's word."

"A court will need something more."

"We have no need of your law here. We live by God's word. We fight His battles daily."

"Not everyone would agree with you."

Eldredge dropped the book into his pocket. "I know what they say about us. That we take wives only to satisfy our lust. But we do God's bidding. We follow His truth on polygamy as it was spoken to the prophet Joseph Smith in the beginning. 'For behold, I reveal unto you a new and everlasting covenant; and if ye abide not that covenant, then are ye damned; for no one can reject this covenant and be permitted to enter into my glory.' Do you understand me now? There is no time limit on *everlasting*. The Mormon Church is damned for turning its back on its own prophet. I say martyrdom here and now is better than giving in to heathen law. That's why we intend to make our stand in Glory."

He stepped to the tunnel mouth and cupped hands around his mouth. "Come, my children. Join us."

Traveler heard what sounded like a whispered chorus of "Amen." Followed by the sound of footsteps.

A moment later women and children began emerging from the mine. Soot-blackened as they were, they reminded him of coal miners he'd seen pictured in history books. The only thing lacking was picks and shovels and lighted helmets.

He counted twenty-one women and about as many children. If the Flock of Zion believed in equal shares, six men divided into twenty-one came out to three-point-five wives apiece.

The women and children wore ragtag clothes. Odds and ends of material that had been stitched together into shapeless garments. The Flock was as much in need of money as Pepper Dalton.

They crowded around the fire pit. Traveler found himself hemmed in next to the flames. Eldredge faced him from the other side of the fire. There was silence. Not so much as a sniffle from the children. Only hostile stares.

"It might be better if we spoke alone somewhere," Traveler said.

"You're not listening to me," Eldredge replied. The strength of his voice caused the flames to flicker. "A flock moves as one. We of the Flock of Zion are one being. What is said to one is said to all."

"Where were you and Priscilla Dalton married?"

"You disappoint me, Brother Traveler. That's such an obvious trap."

Shaking his head, Eldredge began moving among his followers. He laid hands upon them as he went. The touch brought a glow to the women's eyes.

After making the circuit, he came to rest beside Traveler. The crowd rearranged itself so that six women stood out from the others.

"I quote from the good book. 'Seven women shall take hold of one man, saying: we will eat our own bread, and wear our own apparel; only let us be called by thy name to take away our reproach.' These six are also my wives. Do you ask me where they were married?"

So much for equality, Traveler thought. Seven from twenty-one left fourteen. Fourteen women divided by the remaining five men worked out to fewer than three wives apiece.

"Don't bother answering," Eldredge went on. "I know what you're after. If I myself performed the marriage ceremony with Priscilla, then our marriage is void under Gentile law. And if that's so, I cannot inherit her half of Glory."

His head swung from side to side, picking up speed until speech stopped it. "We were married by a justice of the peace in Nevada. I have the paper to prove it."

He retrieved *The Book of Mormon* from his pocket. "I use it as my marker."

With a flourish he removed the limp folded paper and held it out. When Traveler reached for it, the man snatched it back and continued. "The question now is whether or not polygamy—or bigamy, as the likes of you would see it—invalidates this marriage."

He replaced the marker in the book. "There are no other papers like this one, I assure you. That makes me an adulterer by your law, but still Priscilla's rightful heir. Half of Glory belongs to me. To my flock. Think of it. The name of this place is no accident. God caused it to be named Glory. Any man who would put a price on it, the way Pepper Dalton has done, is the devil incarnate."

"Would the devil allow himself to be arrested for murder?" Traveler asked.

Eldredge leaned forward, teetering on tiptoe momentarily before poking a finger against Traveler's chest to catch his balance. "God won't be mocked, not in the presence of His flock, not by the likes of you. We don't care how big or tough you are. So was Goliath. Look what happened to him."

"Is that a threat?"

"From God, not me."

Traveler took a deep breath. Surrounded as he was, confrontation was the last thing he wanted. "I didn't mean to sound sacrilegious."

Eldredge dropped back on his heels. "I'm the one who should apologize. Ever since I heard about Priscilla, guilt has been with me. There is no other word for it. I am responsible for her death."

Traveler tensed. If the man confessed, Traveler wouldn't be allowed out of there, not alive anyway.

From deep underground came the sound of a muffled explosion. The earth shook, hard enough to start a few of the women praying aloud. Eldredge lost his balance and tumbled against Traveler. A blast of heat surged from the tunnel mouth, followed by a puff of black smoke.

"His hunger grows," Eldredge said, righting himself. He gestured toward the mine shaft.

More likely another gas pocket, Traveler answered to himself.

"Women are God's vessels," Eldredge went on. "And man's, to carry his children. They cook and sew and rear the young and obey their husbands. That is their duty. That is the only reason God put them here on earth. But Priscilla, rest her soul, had eaten the forbidden fruit of knowledge before I met her. She'd gone to the university looking for answers."

His teeth clenched; his eyes glared. "Women must look to heaven for their rewards. Here on earth they must be content with necessities only."

He laid a hand on Traveler's arm. "Come, Brother Traveler. Enough of this. Prove that you aren't our enemy. Do battle with us here and now."

Gently but firmly, he steered Traveler through the crowd and toward the opening in the earth. As they stepped inside, Traveler noticed teethlike stalactites hanging from the ceiling. They gnawed on the reflected firelight.

Traveler glanced over his shoulder to see the others falling in behind. He tried to stop but Eldredge tugged at him and said, "Our equipment is just ahead."

The tunnel turned suddenly to reveal half a dozen kerosine lanterns standing on boxes labeled DYNAMITE. Next to them was a green plastic trash container.

While one of the other men began lighting lanterns, Eldredge removed the container's tight-fitting lid and dipped a hand inside. He came up with a fistful of tobacco.

Tobacco, Traveler remembered from Sunday school drill, *is not for the body, neither for the belly.*

Eldredge spoke as if reading his mind. "New words have come to me. The Lord has given tobacco back to us to help sustain us in our trials."

Eldredge loaded his mouth. One after the other, his male followers did the same. They chewed slowly, like cows on cud, waiting for Traveler to join them. The women and children stood back a ways, saying nothing. One of the women opened and closed her mouth in what appeared to be sympathetic chewing.

"It is required," Eldredge said finally.

Traveler tucked a pinch into his mouth. Something stronger would have suited him better.

Eldredge took one lantern and handed another to Traveler. The light from them revealed a gradual slope down into the earth.

Eldredge led the way, moving slowly. He spoke as he went.

"In the beginning Brigham Young wouldn't allow mining. His people's calling, he said, was to farm and raise families, not seek riches. But there are always those who won't listen. They came here and unleashed the fires of hell, Brother Traveler. This mine has been burning ever since, for nearly a century now. Recently it's been getting worse. New fissures open all the time. Flames shoot out of the ground. Many of the old houses in town have been destroyed. We never know if we'll be safe in our beds at night."

"Then why do you stay?"

Eldredge gave no indication that he'd heard the question. "The venting steam is hot enough to scald you to death. Lately we've been driving pipes into the ground to ease the buildup of underground pressure. But nothing seems to help."

He stopped abruptly, reaching out to restrain Traveler with one hand and raising his lantern in the other. Someone bumped into Traveler from behind.

Ahead of them hung a black curtain of smoke. It rose from a fissure in the floor of the tunnel and disappeared into a matching cleft in the stalactite-covered ceiling above.

"This opened two days ago," Eldredge said. "Before that, we could go on for nearly a mile."

"Why would you want to?" Traveler asked.

"The flames have been kindled by Satan as my test. Only by extinguishing them will I earn the right to call myself the True Prophet. The One Picked by God. Only then will Glory become His new Zion, His promised land. But Satan waits for me beyond this barrier. He calls to me in the night, daring me to cross over."

"It's never a good idea to fight the enemy on his own ground," Traveler said.

"Yet you came among us." Eldredge chuckled and gave Traveler a playful nudge toward the smoky chasm.

Hands touched Traveler's back. He braced himself, waiting for the shove.

"Shall the two of us cross over together, Brother Traveler, and meet Satan head-on?"

In desperation, Traveler dredged a long-ago Sunday school lesson from his memory. "'Satan is abroad in the land, and he goeth forth deceiving the nations.'"

"And not here, you mean. Very good, Brother Traveler. But you forget one thing. The word of God as given to His one true prophet, Joseph Smith. 'Wherefore I will say unto them—depart from me, ye cursed, into everlasting fire, prepared for the devil and his angels.' So you see. This is where we'll find him. Are you ready?"

Eldredge raised his hand. Traveler didn't realize it was a signal, not a gesture, until something struck him in the back. He turned in time to see two woman swinging large lumps of coal at him. Pain exploded inside his skull, blinding him. He felt himself start to sag. Hands caught hold of him.

A brittle voice, like something broadcast along a taut string, buzzed in his ear. "Don't hit him again, for Christ's sake. He's too heavy to carry."

"Tie his hands and don't take the Lord's name in vain again."

Cartilage popped in Traveler's shoulder sockets as his arms were wrenched behind him. His wrists caught fire from whatever bound him. The fresh pain revived him enough to start him struggling.

"Help me," a woman shouted.

Someone knocked his feet out from under him. Once he was down, they began kicking him.

"Wait," Eldredge said. "I want to enjoy this by the light of day."

They dragged him up the tunnel and out of the building, where the rain had turned into cinder-colored snow. Traveler's body steamed in the chill air.

Two men, one holding on to each arm, forced Traveler onto his knees in the dirty slush.

Eldredge stepped in front of him to say, "You'd do well to pray while you have the chance, Brother Traveler. But before you do, I want to give you a message for Pepper Dalton, or whoever else you work for. Glory is ours. We'll fight anyone who tries to take it away from us. The mining companies say there's only one way to fight this fire, and that's by gouging open the land. By strip-mining."

His head shook. "If they do that, they'll set loose the demons of hell."

Traveler looked around him, at the faces of the Flock of Zion. "I'd say they were loose already."

Eldredge came at him like a placekicker. His toe caught Traveler in the groin. Traveler's body spasmed face-forward into the tainted snow. Slush filled his mouth. The bile in his throat turned gritty.

He fell onto his side, and Eldredge kicked him again, this time in the mouth. The others joined in.

Traveler didn't realize the kicking had stopped until Eldredge said, "By spilling your blood here today, we've helped you atone for your sins."

Hands grabbed hold of Traveler and dragged him to the Jeep.

"If you come back, you'll atone with your life. Now get out."

Somehow Traveler selected the four-wheel-drive and started the engine. He didn't pass out until he parked by the wall that sheltered the graves of Aunt Libby's beloved dogs.

25

THE DRIVE DOWN from the plateau took hours. Traveler
didn't remember much of it. By the time he parked in front
of Kate Ferguson's house it was close to midnight. The
windows were dark. The thought crossed his mind that he
ought to drive on to a motel, that he wouldn't be welcome
at such an hour.

He was about to restart the engine when his vision
blurred. That had been happening off and on since leaving Glory. Each time, he'd pulled over to the side of the
road to wait for his eyes to clear. Concussion was his
diagnosis. He'd suffered them before while playing football.

After a moment, he opened the door and swung his legs
out of the Jeep. It was the first time he'd moved in some
time. Sudden dizziness toppled him against the fender.
Pain blossomed from his battered ribcage. His eyes wa-
tered. A worm of nausea twisted in his gut, then came
crawling up his throat bent on escape.

He swallowed convulsively and eased onto what passed
for a running board. His head sank down between his
knees. Air whistled through his swollen nose.

By the time he was ready to move again, memory told
him he'd made a mistake. Kate had said she was driving to

Salt Lake to see Pepper. That meant he'd have to go to a motel after all.

He raised his head. Her car was still parked in the driveway. Come to think of it, that made sense. There would have been plenty of time for her to complete a round-trip.

His own trip to the front door reminded him of just how battered and stiff he was. Knocking on the door jarred his head enough to make him wince.

Traveler leaned against the jamb and closed his eyes, waiting for the sound of footsteps, for the porch light to come on. He imagined Kate in a bathrobe, something soft. She'd take him in her arms and comfort him. She'd open the robe and . . .

He jerked himself upright and knocked again, harder. The sound shattered the night. When nothing happened he tried the door and found it locked.

That could be her second car parked there in the driveway, he decided, left behind whenever she went away. The thought made him dizzy again, because it meant no rest for the moment, no comfort. Certainly no bathrobe.

If he could only lie down for a few minutes. That would make all the difference. He thought of the perfectly good couch inside that was going to waste. Surely she wouldn't begrudge him that. Of course not, he told himself, and applied pressure to the door. But it was one of those solid pioneer models, without any give to it at all.

He left the porch, moving slowly in the darkness, and made his way around to the back of the house. There, the screen door was unlatched. The inner door stood open.

"Anybody home?" He crossed the threshold and groped for a light switch. Hairs prickled on the back of his neck a moment before his fingers found the switch.

Kate was hanging upside down from one of the ceiling timbers. For an instant her waxen face appeared to have two mouths. Then Traveler realized that her throat had been cut. He clenched his teeth to keep from screaming his anger.

The cross-beam, head high for him, was low enough to allow Kate's arms to dangle in a puddle of her own blood. Some of it had been used to draw an A on her forehead.

He knew that mark for what it was. A for atonement. Blood atonement as preached by Brigham Young and his followers, handed down through the years to the likes of Zeke Eldredge.

Shaking, Traveler backed out of the kitchen and headed for Kate's only neighbor there at the edge of town. The blue aura of color television was glowing through lace curtains next door. When he knocked, white light washed it away.

The curtains fluttered.

"Who are you?" a woman called from behind them.

"A detective."

"You can't fool me. Fillmore's not big enough to have detectives. All we've got's a sheriff."

"I'm a private detective." Traveler held his ID up against the window glass.

The curtains parted enough to produce a peephole.

"What's your name?" she said. "I can't read small print like that."

"Moroni Traveler."

"Just a minute."

The gray-haired woman who opened the door wore a knitted afghan over her shoulders. She was elderly, well into her seventies, but not the least bit frail. She nudged spectacles along the ridge of her nose to get a better look at him through the screen door.

"I wouldn't normally open up this time of night, young man. But seeing as how you're named Moroni . . . Besides, I saw you go into Katie's place yesterday. Not that I'm a busybody, you understand. It's just that we look out for each other."

"Did you see anybody there today?"

"Katie's business is her own. Besides, when a man comes around in the middle of the night looking like you do, a woman doesn't know what to think. Were you in some kind of accident?"

"More or less."

"Coming from a man your size, that means a fight. Is Katie involved?"

When he didn't answer, her eyes widened. "Something's happened to her. I should have realized that the first time I saw your face. There's more than bruises showing there."

"I'd better call the sheriff," Traveler said.

She unlatched the screen door and started out onto the porch. "Kate will be needing me."

He gently barred her way.

"She's dead, isn't she?"

"I'm afraid so."

Her spectacles fogged.

"Could I have a glass of water?" he said. "Mrs. . . . ?"

"Edna. Everybody calls me Aunt Edna." She brushed her glasses onto her forehead and wiped her eyes with her fingers. "Come in. The phone's there by the TV."

As soon as he was inside the house, the woman disappeared through the nearest doorway. After a moment he heard water running. He sank into a chair imprinted with the old woman's body. The smell of toilet water roses engulfed him.

He picked up the phone, dialed the operator and asked for Sheriff Emmett Culverwell. When the man came on the line Traveler told him where he was and what had happened.

"Two minutes," Culverwell said. "No more. Don't move until I get there."

Edna returned the moment Traveler hung up. She was carrying two glasses of wine. Her eyes were as red as the liquid.

"I brought something stronger than water," she said. "It's elderberry. Some folks say it's not against the Word of Wisdom for medicinal purposes."

He sipped tentatively.

"I hope it's not too sweet."

It was, but warmed his stomach just the same.

A siren wailed in the distance.

"The damn fools will wake the whole town," she said.

"I'd like to ask you some questions," Traveler said.

"I know what's going on. You being here with the sheriff on his way means someone killed my Katie. That's it, isn't it?"

"Yes."

"What do you want to know?"

"Did you see anyone next door today? Anyone suspicious?"

"One of those damned muttonheads, by the look of her."

"I don't understand."

"The polygamists who live up in the mountains. They call themselves the Lambs of God or some such nonsense. Muttonheads, I call them. Dressing like pioneers. This one here today was like all the others, wearing gingham and trying to look like one of Brigham Young's wives."

"What time was that?"

"It was just getting dark but I saw her clearly enough."

"Are you certain it was a woman?" Traveler asked, thinking of Zeke Eldredge, wanting him.

"I'm not blind, young man."

"Was there anyone with her?"

"There could have been a dozen of them in that van," she said. "But if there was I didn't see them."

Traveler thought of the battered minivans in Glory. "What kind of van was it?"

"Like I said, it was getting dark. But I could see that it was banged up some. It was covered with mud, too."

The sheriff's car shrieked to a stop next door.

Traveler made a quick collect call to his father, explaining the situation.

"When will I see you?" Martin asked.

"I'm in no condition to drive at the moment," Traveler said, so his condition wouldn't come as a complete shock. "I ran into Zeke Eldredge and his friends. A few bruises, that's all. At the worst a mild concussion."

"I knew it. You can't mess with religion, not in this state."

"God had nothing to do with what happened."

26

TRAVELER SPENT THE NEXT hour or so waiting in the Jeep. He had an armed, nervous-looking volunteer deputy for company.

"We wouldn't want a guest like yourself getting lonely," Sheriff Culverwell had declared when he'd arrived. "So Jimmy here has agreed to hold your hand until I can devote more time to you personally."

But Jimmy was sitting in the backseat with his hands holding on to a .357.

"Is there any chance of coffee?" Traveler asked the deputy when boredom finally got the better of him.

"Not until I'm relieved."

Traveler leaned back against the plastic headrest, closed his eyes, and thought about Kate Ferguson, trying to remember how she'd looked alive. But the image that came to him was of her hanging upside down.

He switched to Zeke Eldredge, imagining an A etched on the man's forehead. They still had the firing squad for executions in Utah, Traveler reminded himself. A holdover from the days of blood atonement, if historians were to be believed. The thought failed to cheer him.

His eyes snapped open. Body heat had fogged the Jeep's windows. Traveler wiped a hole in the windshield and peered out. Kate's house blazed with light. The only movement came from shadows against the curtains.

He rolled down the window an inch or so, savoring the fresh, cool air. Breathe deeply, he told himself, relax. He leaned back once more and closed his eyes.

Seemingly without transition, he was asleep and dreaming that he was a boy again. It was the night of Pepper Dalton's home run. The three of them—Traveler, his father, and Willis Tanner—were waiting outside Derks Field, hoping to get Pepper's autograph. It was late, nearly midnight, when the shortstop came out of the clubhouse. By then all the other fans had gone home.

"You're my favorite Bee," Traveler said shyly.

"Mine too," Willis put in.

"They want your autograph," Martin explained.

Pepper signed Willis's program first. But while he was doing that, Traveler panicked. He'd thrown his program away.

He tugged on his father's arm and whispered, "Do you have any paper?"

Martin searched his pockets and wallet, but without success.

In desperation Traveler took off his baseball cap and handed it to the shortstop. Pepper signed on the light blue brim.

Someone rapped on the window. Traveler woke up wondering whatever happened to that cap.

"The rule of thumb," Sheriff Culverwell said when Traveler had lowered the glass, "is the husband or boyfriend did it."

"In case you've forgotten, Pepper Dalton is still in jail in Salt Lake."

"Could be you fall into the latter category." He shook a finger at Traveler's face. "Could be she gave you that black eye and those bruises."

Traveler stretched. It was a mistake. Jimmy jabbed a pistol barrel in the back of his neck.

"You'd better step out," the sheriff said, though it wasn't certain whether he meant Traveler or the deputy.

They both got out of the car. The area was illuminated by headlights from three vehicles, one an ambulance that had been angled to face the front of the house. All had engines running to keep their batteries charged.

"It's all right, Jimmy," the sheriff said. "I'll handle him now. In the meantime you see if the doctor needs a hand inside with the body bag."

Jimmy nodded, trying to look like an old hand at murder. But his face gave him away. He reminded Traveler of a boy on his first date.

As soon as the deputy disappeared around the side of the house, Culverwell took Traveler by the arm and led him up the front walk. The stark light had bleached all color from the concrete underfoot.

Culverwell said, "There's something I want you to look at up here on the porch. Be careful where you step."

The porch consisted of a low concrete slab, no more than three feet wide and six feet long. Half a dozen dark blotches, like Rorschachs, stained it. A partial footprint showed in one of the stains.

"I didn't notice them when I walked up here in the dark," Traveler said.

He raised one foot and then the other. The same dark material was wedged into the tread of one sole. Traveler slipped off the shoe and took a whiff.

"Tobacco," Culverwell said for him. "You wouldn't happen to chew, would you?"

Traveler grimaced to show stain-free teeth. "It's like I said before, Sheriff. Zeke Eldredge. Or one of his followers. They all chew the damn stuff. They say God has given them a new revelation on the subject."

"So I've heard." The sheriff made a show of cringing. "It's even been used to justify all the chewing that goes on among members of Pepper's baseball team."

"Eldredge is a violent man. I have the bruises to prove it."

"Someone's bringing him in for questioning right now."

"I'd like to be there when you talk to him."

"That I can't allow. It would violate his rights, and my conscience."

"You say that like a bishop, not a sheriff."

"I used to think I could keep one job separate from the other. But the older I get the less able I am to cope. Even on one level."

Culverwell knelt down to touch a spot of tobacco. "It's still wet."

"Have you taken samples?"

"Even in Fillmore we know enough to do that. They tell me you can get blood type from spit these days. Of course there's no guarantee that this tobacco has anything to do with Kate's murder."

"I've never met a cop who liked coincidences," Traveler said.

The sheriff studied his dirty finger for a moment before rubbing it in the grass. "You'd be locked up right now if we'd found chewing tobacco on you."

"Somehow I don't think I'm one of your suspects."

"Aren't you?" The sheriff's knees popped when he got to his feet. "Kate asked me to perform her wedding ceremony. Did you know that? It couldn't have been a temple wedding, not until they were both accepted into the church in good standing, but I was still happy for her."

A long sigh deflated him. He gulped air in order to continue speaking. "She should have married a long time ago. I told her that, too, when I agreed to perform the service. Passion is for the young, I told her. Do you know what she said to that?"

He paused, shaking his head to forestall an answer. "She said, 'I didn't meet Pepper when I was young.'"

His head continued its protesting movement. "I sometimes think that when we get older we just go through the motions. Even when it comes to marriage and sex. By middle age we're running on automatic pilot. The memories we've stored in our youth are what see us through. That's what life is all about, you know. Memories. They hold you together when everything else fails. I told Kate just that, that she and Pepper wouldn't have any memories to share."

A door slammed at the rear of the house. A moment later two men came out of the side yard bearing the bagged body on an old-fashioned stretcher, one without wheels.

"If I ever find out that you had anything to do with this—" The sheriff broke off to blow his nose.

"I know," Traveler said. "I feel the same way."

27

A DAWN WAKE-UP CALL got Traveler out of the Paradise
Motel in time to reach Salt Lake for a late breakfast. But by
then his father had already left the house.

A letter-length note, unusual for Martin, was propped
against the cornflakes box on the kitchen table.

Mo,

When the phone rings in the middle of the night like
that, an old man like me thinks the worst. You get up figuring someone's dead. Or hurt maybe. Your heart pounds all
the way to the damned phone. You can hardly breathe
when you get there.

Of course, I was worried about you, so hearing from
you was fine. Only a mild concussion, you said, as if I was
to go back to bed and forget all about it. But that's easier
said than done, especially at my age when a man needs all
the sleep he can get. The curse of being a parent is never
hearing from your children when you want to. Only when
they find the time to think about you. Or need money or
bail.

Anyway, I waited around here as long as I could this
morning to see that concussion for myself, but someone has

to keep Moroni Traveler & Son open. Or should I say Moroni Traveler & Son and Son?

Which brings me to Claire. I found an envelope from her under the door when I got home. It contained the Monopoly card you'll find on the mantel. She also called last night, at a decent hour for her, and left a message. She says, quote: 'I know Moroni found my first clue. Now we have to talk about it. You tell him that for me.'

Though why she wants to talk to you, I can't understand. After all, I'm the father of her child, aren't I? It says so right on the subpoena.

In any case, she left a number for you. I jotted it down on the pad next to the phone. You'll also find Chuck Cecil's number there. He called again, collect, and I accepted, only I didn't know what to ask him exactly, though I figured it had something to do with Hap Kilgore. All we did was talk about the old days when he played center field for the Bees. He seemed pleased that somebody remembered him after all these years.

Martin

Traveler read the note through again, sighed, and called the office. The answering machine said, "Hello. You've reached Moroni Traveler and Son . . . and Son. None of us can come to the phone right now, so leave your message after the beep."

Traveler waited until it was time to say, "Dad, I'll see you for dinner if not sooner," and disconnected.

His head was aching again, not as bad as last night, but enough to make him sensitive to the light streaming in through the window next to the telephone nook.

His next call was to the Stratford Hotel in Baltimore. Chuck Cecil wasn't in his room. Traveler left a message.

He was halfway through the sequence of Claire's

number when he changed his mind and hung up. Talking to her on the phone never got him anywhere. Then again, he couldn't see her in person if he didn't play by her rules.

Frustrated, he retrieved her Monopoly card from the mantel. It said COMMUNITY CHEST on the front and depicted a man holding two newly born babies. A nurse stood next to him holding her hand out to be paid. Bold black printing said PAY HOSPITAL $100. On the back Claire had written "play the game for your next clue."

Traveler shook his head. A feeling of exhaustion swept over him. He thought about going to bed for the rest of the day, but his conscience wouldn't allow it. A shower and a change of clothes would have to do.

While the water was running to warm up, he swallowed three aspirin and shaved. After that, he soaked under the spray until the hot water ran out. By then the headache was gone.

The clothes he selected, tan slacks and maroon crewneck sweater, had been birthday gifts from Claire. The brown, penny-free loafers had been his choice. He slipped them on while dialing her number.

"My angel," she said as soon as she heard his voice. "I've been praying that you'd call."

He held his breath, listening for background noise, for any sign that he'd reached her at one of her usual hangouts. This time there was nothing but the static created by her lips rubbing against the mouthpiece.

"You're a good detective, Moroni. But even you need clues."

As always her breathless telephone voice brought back bedroom memories from when he'd lived with her after moving back to Salt Lake from Los Angeles.

"Don't you think Monopoly cards are a bit obvious?" he said.

"Oh, Mo. Don't you remember how we played the

game? The special rules we had? What I used to do to you with my mouth whenever you lost?"

"I remember."

"You used to lose on purpose, didn't you? Come on. Admit it."

"I don't have much time, Claire."

"I know for a fact that you had time to come looking for me at my old apartment. They told me so."

"I was doing it for my father."

"Exactly." She spoke the word with triumph.

"I'm going to hang up."

"I can always tell when you're lying, Moroni. Always."

"What do you really want, Claire?"

"A name for my child. Our child."

"It's not mine."

"Oh, yes, Moroni. I was thinking of you at the moment I conceived it. I closed my eyes, opened my legs and thought of you doing it to me. When I came I screamed your name. It's yours, all right."

Jesus, he thought, the conversation reminded him of something he'd overheard as a child. Something between his mother and Martin.

"Why sue my father for paternity then?"

"I knew you'd fight me if I tried that with you."

"And you think my father won't?"

"I know you. You'll marry me to protect his name."

28

Traveler daydreamed about the Monopoly games he'd played with Claire. The prizes that went with Boardwalk and Park Place, her sensuous reward for passing Go, and what she called her special ride on the Reading Railroad. But what haunted him most was her smile. No real joy in it, only mockery.

He tried a smile of his own. The muscles around his mouth felt stiff and unused. He tested them again in the bathroom mirror. There was nothing funny about the bruises on his face. They'd turned yellow, tinged with green around the edges. The colors matched the way he felt.

Grimacing, he fingered the Community Chest card. The nurse depicted there reminded him that Claire had once checked herself into the hospital for observation. Was that where she was now, giving birth to Moroni Traveler the third?

He turned the card over and reread Claire's note. Sooner or later he would have to follow her instructions and play the game. In the meantime, the Monopoly nurse reminded him of something else, that he had work to do at the Phoebe Clinton Home.

Ten minutes later he drove up the circular driveway and

parked under the porte cochere. On his first trip there, thunderheads had been spilling over the Wasatch Mountains. Today the sky was fiercely blue.

The house stood on the high ground of Twelfth East. From the porch he could see all the way to the Great Salt Lake. He could smell it, too, the rotten-egg taint of pollution carried on a west wind.

He walked into a two-story entrance hall that still had the look of an 1880s mansion, walnut woodwork, Doric columns of marble, and a grand Gothic staircase. The pattern on the flocked wallpaper, fleur-de-lis, showed through despite a coat of white paint that had aged to the color of old teeth. Pine-scented air freshener failed to mask the underlying odor of decay.

"Hello," Traveler called. His voice echoed across the granite floor, Utah granite as cold and uninviting as the facade of the Mormon temple itself.

The granite magnified each footstep as he crossed the hall to the base of the staircase, which rose to a second-floor landing before branching both left and right. Above the landing was a massive stained-glass window, where an inlaid Doubting Thomas had his finger buried in Christ's wound.

Traveler was starting up the stairs when someone coughed behind him. Feeling like he'd been caught prying, he turned to see Golly Simpson. At the sight of Traveler's face, the man's smile faltered, but quickly righted itself to become as crisp and bright as the white uniform he wore.

"I'm sorry," he said. "I didn't hear you come in."

White letters on his blue plastic name tag said: G. SIMPSON, STAFF.

"I'm here to see Hap Kilgore," Traveler said.

"By golly, I am sorry. We do love having visitors come to see our residents. But you've missed him. He doesn't usually get back from the ballpark much before supper-time."

"It was my understanding that he no longer worked for the Saints baseball team."

"That can't be right, Mr. . . . ?"

"Have you forgotten me already? Moroni Traveler. The man you were spying on at Derks Field."

"As you can see, I work here."

"The owner of the Saints, Jessie Gilchrist, seems to think you work for him. He tells me that you're some kind of talent scout. But scouts don't usually watch their own teams through binoculars from the left field bleachers when they can sit in the dugout. The way I figure it is, I'm the one you're scouting."

"As I said, Hap Kilgore isn't here. I suggest you call ahead next time."

"Just what is your job here, Simpson? Are you spying on Hap Kilgore by any chance?"

"That's a laugh."

"All right. Tell me what 'staff' means then."

"In my case, by golly, it means I own the place . . . with my sister."

"I didn't know Phoebe Clinton was still alive," Traveler said.

"Her name is Mary Cook and you know it, though some call her Mother Mary."

Traveler remembered her, the capable heavyset woman he'd talked to on the day he brought Hap home from the ballpark.

Mrs. Cook's office was a converted solarium with glass walls on three sides. One of them was trapping the spring sun and redirecting it onto Traveler, causing him to sweat.

From behind a desk occupying the only shade in the room, she pointed an accusing finger at him. "When we first met, Mr. Traveler, you told me that you were trying to help Hap Kilgore."

"That's correct."

"And my brother? Are you helping him too? Without his knowledge?"

Traveler adjusted his chair to get the sun out of his eyes. Once he didn't have to squint, he decided that Mrs. Cook, with her gray hair and shiny, makeup-free face, had to be somewhere in her late fifties.

"To be frank, Mrs. Cook, or would you prefer Mother Mary. . . ?"

"I would not."

". . . I caught your brother spying on us at the ballpark."

"Don't talk to me about being frank, Mr. Traveler. I have a very good memory. I remember exactly what you said the last time you were here. That you were a detective working for Mr. Kilgore, but that there wasn't any trouble. Or doesn't a man in your profession consider murder trouble?"

"When I said that, I meant that Hap wasn't in trouble."

"What other hidden meanings were there in that conversation we had?"

"Hap hired me, Mrs. Cook, not you. My first duty is to him."

For the first time since he'd entered the woman's office, she relaxed and smiled. She picked up a silver picture frame from her desk and turned it around so that Traveler could see it. Hap was younger then, in a Bees uniform. The inscription read, "With all my love, Hap."

"I feel the same way myself. Hap comes first with me, too. He's asked me to marry him."

"That's one thing he didn't tell me."

"That's my Hap all right. He thinks he's protecting my honor by keeping it a secret until we're actually married. But I think we're already an item around here."

She turned away, but not before he'd seen her blush. "It's not just my office that's a fishbowl," she said. "There's no privacy in a place like this. You see, a lot of our residents have trouble sleeping, so we allow them kitchen privileges to fix themselves cocoa at night. All that roaming around occasionally leads to mischief. The spreading of rumors on the bathroom walls, for one thing. Judging from some of the more recent messages, Hap must have been seen coming out of my room."

"Does your brother live here?"

"Technically speaking, only staff and residents have live-in privileges. But I'll admit it. I do keep a small room for Golly."

Traveler wiped sweat out of his eyes. "I was telling the truth before, Mrs. Cook. I did see your brother watching me and Hap at the ballpark."

"Call me Mary, please."

He nodded that he would.

"What can I say about Golly?" she said. "To him, I'll always be the little sister who needs protecting. He's probably keeping an eye on Hap to be certain that he makes an honest woman out of me."

"Your brother also followed us to a coffee shop. Hap saw him there, but said he didn't recognize him. Why would he do that?"

"I can't explain, not unless Hap was embarrassed to find himself being spied on by his future brother-in-law."

"What does your brother do for a living?"

"That's not an easy question to answer, though he does manage to do a few odd jobs around here for me once in a while."

"Does he have anything to do with the Saints baseball team?"

She sighed deeply. "Golly means well. He loves baseball and he wants to be knowledgeable because of Hap's expertise. But I don't think he has any kind of formal position. Actually, Golly likes to call himself an entrepreneur, an investment counselor. But the Phoebe Clinton Home is the only investment he ever made, and that was with the money our parents left us. Take a look around you. It's obvious to anyone that we're about to go bust."

Traveler glanced away from the misery on the woman's face. In so doing, he noticed how many of the panes in the solarium windows were cracked. All were dirty.

"Let me assure you," she continued, "that we do our best to keep the place up. But what money we have is best used for heating and the proper nutrition of our residents. Not frills like fixing windows and repainting every little worn spot."

He remembered the fresh coat of paint out front, the one that didn't extend to the sides or back of the mansion.

"That's why Hap tried to get back into baseball. He wanted to bring in some extra money to help pay the bills. He would have, too, if Pepper Dalton's plans had worked out. Pepper was going to make Hap a coach, you know."

"It may still happen."

"Dear God. Making Hap a coach was only part of it. 'I owe everything to you,' Pepper told my Hap. I was there when he said it. 'You stuck by me in the old days, when they wanted to dump me off the Bees for hitting less than my weight. I'll never forget that,' he said. 'Half of everything I inherit is going to be yours eventually. Half ownership in the team, our new Bees. You'll be more than my coach, Hap. Eventually you'll be my general manager.' Those were his words. After all these years, Hap's dream was going to come true. He was going to be part of baseball again. And in the front office, too."

"That's wonderful."

"That was then. Now is now. The state inspectors are

due next week. There's a good chance we won't pass the inspection. If that happens my dream of helping the elderly will die. Where will Hap and I be then? We'll both be out of work, that's what. Depending on how the trial goes of course. Depending on what you do to help Pepper, to help all of us out of this mess."

"Hap didn't tell me he was going to be a partner."

"He's not a man to blow his own horn."

She left her desk to rub a peephole in one of the grimy panes. Peering out she said, "I love this place. My grandfather, Jedediah Simpson, built it. Golly's real name is Jedediah, but he's never gone by it."

She turned away from the window to take Traveler's hand. "Come on. Let me introduce you to Jed." There was an astringent smell to her, part medicinal, part female.

Together they returned to the entrance hall and climbed the staircase to the landing. Beneath the stained-glass Doubting Thomas hung a gold-framed portrait. A plaque attached to the frame was inscribed "Jedediah Simpson, 1910."

"Grandfather couldn't read or write but he knew silver when he saw it. He struck it rich in Park City in 1883. He owned half the town before he was done."

Her eyes closed, her hands pressed together as if in prayer. "Eventually the land came to my father. By then, however, Park City was a ghost town. Dad, Jed Junior, spent his life trying to bring it back to life. Unfortunately for him, he thought a new vein of silver was the only way to do it. In the end, he sold out to developers who made millions by turning Park City into a ski resort. I think that's what killed him, not having the vision to see the riches that were right there in front of him all the time. I watched him die, Mr. Traveler, and I couldn't help. That's when I decided to become a nurse. The Phoebe Clinton Home is my way of paying him back. I treat the elderly here as I would my own father."

Her eyes opened. "He left us just enough to buy this place when it came on the market."

"You said this was your brother's folly."

"I confess, Mr. Traveler. I'm as foolish at heart as he is. You can't get rich helping people."

Traveler shifted his gaze to Doubting Thomas. For some reason he felt like poking Mary Cook to see if she was real.

Instead, he clasped his hands behind his back and said, "Do you know Kate Ferguson?"

"No. I don't think so."

"She's Pepper Dalton's fiancée."

"That's right. Now that you say it, I remember Hap mentioning her. Why do you ask?"

"You remind me of her a little," he lied.

As far as he knew, there had been nothing on the radio or in the papers yet about the killing.

"By the way," he said, "your brother told me that Hap went to the ballpark this morning."

"My Hap does that every morning. Like clockwork. We won't see him again till sunset. That man and his baseball. He loves it as much as I do this home."

"Didn't he tell you what happened with the Saints?"

"That they let him go? Of course he did. And him working for nothing. It almost broke his heart. But he said it wasn't going to stop him from keeping an eye on things for Pepper's sake."

"How well do you know Mr. Dalton?"

"He's Hap's best friend."

"And his sister, Priscilla?"

"I met her only once. Pepper brought her here just the other day. The day before she died, I think it was. He wanted her to see the good work that was being done at the home."

"Why would he do that?"

"I'm sorry. I should have explained. I've gone over

this so many times before, both in my mind and to friends, that I sometimes think everybody knows what's going on. You see, she and Pepper are a lot like me and Golly. But with one exception. When we inherited some money, we both agreed on what should be done with it. That we would buy back the family home. But when Priscilla and Pepper inherited land, they fought like cats and dogs. He wanted to sell and she didn't. That's why he brought her here, to show her what Hap's coaching money would be used for."

"And what did she say to that?"

"What could she say? We introduced her to all our old folks. Once she knew them personally, knew that they'd be out on the street if we had to close down the home, she had no choice. She agreed to sell."

29

TRAVELER FOUND HAP KILGORE standing outside Derks Field looking up at the left field fence. He had a fielder's glove on one hand and his Redman pouch in the other.

"They're holding afternoon batting practice," he explained at Traveler's approach.

Traveler cocked his head, listening for the crack of the bat. What he heard was the rush of nearby traffic on Main Street.

"If my Saints keep their eyes on the ball like I taught 'em, home runs ought to be coming my way any minute. All I've got to do is catch three balls and turn them in and I get a free ticket to tonight's game."

Kilgore dipped his mouth into the tobacco pouch without taking his eyes from the fence. His lips puckered to scoop out a mouthful before he returned the pack to his pocket. His hand was then free to remove his cap, an old Bees model, Traveler noticed, with SL stitched on the front instead of the Saints' haloed S.

"The trouble is, I don't know who's up at the plate batting," Kilgore said. "Otherwise I could position myself better." He jabbed a thumb over his shoulder toward Main Street. "If a ball gets past me, it's hell chasing it down in traffic."

He shifted his feet as if to limber up, but nearly lost his balance in the process. It was then Traveler noticed that the old man's face was gray with fatigue.

"For Christ's sake, Hap, why don't you rest for a while? Tickets don't cost that much."

"I've got to save every nickel if I'm going to pay that big-city fee of yours. Speaking of which, maybe it's about time you backed off. Pepper has a good lawyer. You told me so yourself. And I hate to spend money I haven't got."

Kilgore tucked the cap under his arm, liberating a hand to wipe the sweat from his bald head while still keeping his mitt at the ready. A red welt circled his head where the sweatband had been.

"How long have you been waiting out here?" Traveler asked.

"Thirty minutes or so. Since the start of afternoon batting practice. I was unlucky this morning. Only one ball cleared the fence and some kid beat me to it."

"I'll buy you a ticket."

Kilgore replaced the cap, adjusting it carefully until it matched the crease in his head. His glance at Traveler was no more than a twitch. "It's a matter of pride, Mo. I haven't bought my way into a ball game in years. I'm not about to start now."

The echoing sound of a bat connecting with a baseball started Kilgore pounding his glove in expectation. "That sounds like it has some distance."

"I've got it," someone called from inside the park.

"Son of a bitch," Kilgore exploded. "Those guys can't hit shit today. Pepper's going to have to do some house-cleaning when he takes over."

"Left field here is longer than most major league parks. You said so yourself."

"We're talking batting practice, for God's sake. You throw a pitch down the middle and even a hitter like Pepper ought to be able to knock them out of the park occasionally."

"If the Saints are that bad, why waste your time standing here?"

"I told you. It's the principle of the thing. If I don't get any balls this afternoon, I'll wait out front during the next game. There's always a couple of dozen fouled over the grandstand. They're in good condition, too, since they haven't been used for batting practice. Of course the Saints pay a couple of high school kids to retrieve them. They take them away from you if they can."

"How the hell can you compete?"

"They're faster than I am, sure. Stronger, too. But I know the tricks of the trade. Some of the balls end up hidden under cars, or in the storm drains. So don't worry about me. I'll come up with a couple." He kept watching the sky above left field.

"We've got to talk," Traveler said.

Kilgore stiffened, turning slowly toward Traveler for the first time as he spoke. "Is something wrong? Is Pepper . . . Jesus, man, you look awful. What happened to your face?"

"Zeke Eldredge."

"I warned you. That man's dangerous, a goddamned lunatic. Why the police arrested Pepper instead of him I'll never know."

"Let's go somewhere," Traveler said. "I haven't had lunch yet."

"I brown-bagged it so I wouldn't have to leave my post." The old man's eyes started to look away, anxious to be back searching for home runs, when he suddenly caught himself. "Shit. What am I thinking of? You didn't come down here to show me your face. Or talk baseball either." He spit tobacco juice. "I can see it in your eyes. Bad news."

"Kate Ferguson is dead."

A sudden intake of breath sent tobacco down Kilgore's throat and started him choking. Traveler pounded him on the back until the old man flapped his arms to indicate he was all right.

"What happened?" Kilgore croaked.

"She was murdered."

Kilgore coughed and swallowed, then repeated the process. "It has to be Zeke. She was probably doing something to help Pepper and got herself killed."

"I told the sheriff in Fillmore pretty much the same thing, that Eldredge was the logical suspect."

"Christ, I hope I'm wrong," Kilgore went on. "But Pepper has that effect on people. He gets people like Kate to do what he wants without actually asking."

"I don't think you have to worry. As far as I know, she had no contact with Pepper after he was arrested."

"I'm not saying he told her to go out and spy on Zeke Eldredge. But she was Pepper's fiancée, for Christ's sake. He could manipulate her as easily as he did the players on his team. Or maybe motivate is a better word. Whatever you call it, it's a thing with him. He loves being in control. He has these pep talks he uses to win friends and influence people, as they say. Look at me. I wanted to help him but didn't know how. So I did the next best thing. I brought you into it."

"What are you getting at? That Pepper was responsible? By proxy?"

"Christ, who knows? Maybe I've been standing out here in the sun too long."

The loud crack of a bat preceded the appearance of a baseball soaring over the stadium wall. Unnoticed by Hap, it rolled all the way to Main Street.

30

BY THE TIME TRAVELER reached the Chester Building the weather had changed again. Angry-looking thunderheads were sailing across the Wasatch Mountains like prairie schooners following the Mormon Trail. He bypassed his usual parking lot and pulled into the red zone out front.

The lobby was empty except for Nephi Bates standing guard outside his elevator. At Traveler's approach, the man held up his *Book of Mormon* like a vampire hunter confronting Dracula.

Traveler took the stairs. The three flights left him more winded than they should have. He panted into the office and dropped onto the client's chair next to his father's desk.

"Did you get my note?" Martin asked as he set aside the book he'd been reading. Its title was *How to Cope with a New Baby in the House.* Half a dozen other volumes on the same subject were stacked nearby.

Traveler nodded.

Martin slipped off his reading glasses and studied his son's battered face, tilting his head first one way and then the other like an art critic trying to achieve the perfect perspective. "You've looked worse, but that won't keep me from saying I told you so."

"I know. Moroni Traveler and Son's rules for survival."

"Exactly. God and religion don't mix. Now tell me. What does Zeke Eldredge's face look like?"

"I didn't lay a hand on him. I got sucker-punched by one of his wives."

"I'll be goddamned." Martin pressed his lips together, quelling a smile. "Speaking of women, did you call Claire?"

"Yes."

"I hope you asked her when the baby's due?"

"I'm afraid not," Traveler said, still having trouble with his breathing.

"The sound of you tells me the elevator's broken down again."

"No. It's Nephi. He's in one of his moods."

"You know who put him there, don't you? Willis Tanner. He was here less than an hour ago. He's Elton Woolley's personal messenger as far as Nephi's concerned. From Willis's mouth come the words of the president of the church, God's living prophet on earth."

"Considering how close Willis is to Woolley, that's probably true."

"'Behold, I will send my messenger, and he shall prepare the way before me,'" Martin said, quoting scripture as revised by the church's first prophet, Joe Smith.

"Very impressive. Now tell me what Willis had to say."

"That he came in person because he didn't trust the phones. When I heard that, I expected a revelation from God at the very least. What I got was news that Pepper Dalton has been hospitalized with chest pains."

"A heart attack?"

"They don't think so, but they're not taking chances. They've got him under guard at the LDS Hospital. Why would he come here to tell me that?"

"Because I asked Willis to get me in to see Pepper."

"No chance of that now. Willis made a point of saying so."

"I'm stuck, then. There's not much more I can do."

"To begin with, you can help me make some important decisions." Martin slapped a palm down on the how-to books at his elbow. "First, you've got to understand that having a baby isn't like bringing home a new puppy. Things have to be done. The way I see it we can begin by fixing up your room. Of course that's going to leave you out in the cold."

Traveler eased out of his chair to stare at the temple across the street. Its spires looked tall enough to poke holes in the passing thunderheads.

"Naturally, Claire will have to stay there, too, as long as she's nursing."

Every so often his father came up with schemes that would give Traveler an excuse to move out of the house. He did it so Traveler wouldn't feel obliged to stay on and keep an old man company.

"We'll paint over your furniture, either blue or pink depending on the sex of the baby."

"Claire told me it's going to be Moroni the third," Traveler said.

"There are times when I'm certain that woman is related to your mother. When a man gets to be my age he wants grandchildren. He has the need to pass his heritage on to the next generation. Family histories and memories. Everything that makes you immortal."

Traveler crossed the room to his own desk. From there he said, "You haven't told me all the family history yet."

"It's easier with someone you don't know."

"For God's sake." Traveler knew that he wasn't Martin's biological son, that he'd been conceived while Martin was away in the army. But the closest Martin had ever come to admitting it was to say that upbringing was more important than genetics.

Martin said, "If you're not going to give me grandchildren, I'll have to settle for another son."

"In that case you'll want to see this." Traveler handed him the Monopoly card with Claire's note on the back. "As the expectant father, you'll want to start calling the hospitals to find her."

"And what will you be doing?"

"Going home to bed."

"I don't think so. You see, there's something else I haven't told you. The prophet's messenger had something else to say. Two people are being allowed into the hospital to see Pepper Dalton. Hap Kilgore and Dalton's attorney, Sam Howe, who's just been named to head up Deseret Coal and Gas. The same people who want to buy Glory."

31

LATE AFTERNOON SUN SLANTED through a break in the clouds, creating a rainbow in the rain high on the east bench. Traveler judged it to be somewhere near the Phoebe Clinton Home. But he doubted there would be any pot of gold by the time he got there.

He had a stop to make on the way, the Deseret Coal and Gas Company on Second South. Its offices were located in one of those turn-of-the-century red brick, stone-corniced buildings whose grimy past had been sandblasted away to create a fashionable present.

Sam Howe was waiting for him inside, perched on the receptionist's desk in an otherwise deserted outer office.

"Good to see you, Moroni," he said, hopping off the furniture to shake hands enthusiastically. He was nearly a foot shorter than Traveler and spoke without looking up. "I'd make you more comfortable in one of our inner sanctums, but the drones are here going over the books."

"Congratulations," Traveler responded, indicating the premises with a sweep of his hand. "I understand you're in charge now."

"A temporary measure only, I assure you. A matter of reorganization. I like to think of it as a special kind of

Chapter Eleven. Only this is a moral bankruptcy, with me here to protect both the financial and spiritual interests of the creditors." He grinned. "Now, what can I do for you?"

"I need a legal opinion. Wouldn't you say it was a conflict of interest to represent both Pepper Dalton and Deseret Coal at the same time?"

Howe squinted up at Traveler's face before returning to his perch. "A man your size ought to be able to win his battles. But one look at your face tells me you don't know when to back off."

"Is that a warning?"

"Don't misunderstand me. All I'm talking about is conflict of interest, since you brought up the subject. Like what comes first in a man's priorities."

"You mean the church."

"Think about it, Moroni. God put the coal there in Glory for us to use. It's only a question of when and how we choose to mine it."

"You left out the profit to be made."

The attorney shook his head. "I feel sorry for you, Moroni. I really do. The only prophet I'm concerned with is God's—and that's not spelled the same way."

"Zeke Eldredge has been called a prophet."

"It doesn't take a theologian to know that a repentant sinner is always welcome to rejoin the fold."

"Is that your way of saying business is business? That you'll deal with Eldredge if you have to?"

"You and I both represent Pepper Dalton, so you might as well know the truth. He's already signed an agreement of sale with us here at Deseret Coal. That was part of my fee."

"And if he loses in court?"

"When I appear in for the defense, Moroni, people know where I stand. Both judges and juries."

"Humor me. Pretend there's been a travesty of justice and your client has been convicted."

Howe ran a hand through his short, sandy hair. "I'm only a simple lawyer, you understand."

And thirteenth apostle, Traveler reminded himself.

"But it's my opinion that Priscilla Dalton was only one wife among many," he went on. "That makes her no wife at all in the eyes of the law."

"Zeke told me that she was the only woman he ever married legally. He's got a marriage certificate to prove it."

"Bullshit." Howe's teeth snapped as if trying to bite back the obscenity.

"I saw the document myself."

"It's a forgery. It has to be. Priscilla Dalton left no documents behind, no written will. Since her marriage is a fraud, her brother, as next-of-kin, becomes sole owner of the Glory Mine."

"Then you won't mind if I talk to him."

"Be my guest."

"I need your permission."

"For what it's worth, you have it."

Traveler didn't like Howe's tone but didn't figure him for a liar either.

Traveler changed the subject. "Zeke Eldredge is not the kind of man to give up Glory without a fight."

"Then the Lambs of God will be led to slaughter."

32

THERE WAS NO SIGN of a rainbow by the time Traveler reached the Phoebe Clinton Home. Light was fading from the sky. The smell of cabbage leaking all the way to the porte cochere told him dinnertime was near.

He found Hap Kilgore and Mary Cook holding hands on the concrete stoop around back. They broke contact as soon as they saw him. Kilgore, whose normal complexion was red, flushed an even brighter shade than usual. Mary matched his color. The adoring look in her eyes made Traveler envious.

"Mo," Kilgore said, "what brings you here?"

"I just left Sam Howe. He's given me permission to see Pepper."

Mary touched Hap on the arm, a lover's gesture.

"He's already out on bail," she said.

"That's right," Kilgore added. "He called me himself to say that it was all over but the shouting."

"I don't understand," Traveler said.

"I don't know all the details myself. But Pepper told me that his lawyer had done his stuff, and that charges will be dropped and bail refunded any time now."

"We owe it to you, Mr. Traveler," Mary said.

Kilgore nodded his agreement. "Pepper said the same

thing. That you stirring things up in Glory convinced everybody he didn't do it."

"Are they going to arrest Eldredge then?"

"I told you that in the first place. There's no one else it could be."

"I'd still like to talk to Pepper myself," Traveler said.

Kilgore rubbed his bald head before taking hold of Mary's hand again. Their fingers intertwined. "I don't know where he is right now. The fact is, he said he'd be unavailable for the next couple of days. I guess he needs time to get over being locked up."

"When did you talk to him?"

"Not more than an hour ago." Kilgore leaned down to kiss the top of Mary's head. "I guess you know what Pepper being out of jail means? That the Saints will soon be his. As soon as we heard that, Mary put me on a diet."

He rubbed his stomach with his free hand. "I don't want to look like some of these old farts who waddle up and down the coach's box with their stomachs hanging out. No, sir. By the time Pepper names me his third base coach, I'll look the way I used to. A coach has got to be fast on his feet. Otherwise, he could get himself killed by a foul ball."

Kilgore sucked in his stomach, but had to let it out again as soon as he went back to breathing.

"If you had to make a guess," Traveler said, "where would you look for Pepper?"

"The only thing else he said was that he had an eviction order against Zeke Eldredge."

"Are you sure?"

"Pepper's lawyer got to a Mormon judge. You know the kind. They like nothing better than sticking it to polygamists, so they can show the world that the church no longer sanctions such hanky-panky."

"Now, Hap," Mary said. "Just be thankful that everything's going to be all right."

The porch light came on.

"That's the signal for dinner," Mary announced. "Would you care to join us, Mr. Traveler?"

Kilgore made a face. "All I get is vegetables and salad until I lose this stomach."

"It's for your own good," Mary said, then turned her eyes on Traveler. "You could stand to lose a few pounds too, young man."

"I don't think of myself as young."

"It's a matter of perspective," she said to him, though she was smiling at Kilgore.

"Why don't I skip dinner altogether," Kilgore said, "and go to the ball game? Maybe Mo will drive me."

Mary shook a finger at Kilgore. "I don't want you eating hot dogs or drinking beer. Do you hear me?"

"Yes, ma'am." He hung his head for an instant before grabbing hold and hugging her.

"You'll muss my hair," she said with a smile.

He kissed her on the nose.

"I'm counting on you to look after him, Mr. Traveler," she said before retreating inside.

Kilgore didn't speak again until they were in the car. "I should have met her forty years ago. If I had . . ." His head shook. ". . . who knows what might have happened?"

"In case you've forgotten, there's no game tonight."

Grinning, Kilgore pulled his Bees cap from a back pocket and adjusted it on his head. "Hal, the grounds keeper at Derks, is a friend of mine. He's meeting me there so we can do some work on the third base coach's box. It needs manicuring around the edges."

33

DERKS FIELD WAS DARK except for half a dozen low-watt night-lights burning over the ticket windows. Under Kilgore's direction, Traveler maneuvered the car over the curb and along a blacktopped parking area. When he finally came to a stop, the car's headlights were focused on a roll-away metal door that stood between the left field bleachers and the grandstand. There were no other cars parked in the area, no sign of life at all.

"Hal usually leaves it open a crack for me," Kilgore explained.

Traveler saw only a solid wall.

"Could be he's being careful tonight and only left the lock off the hook." Kilgore nodded to himself and got out of the car.

After killing the engine but not the lights, Traveler joined him on the asphalt. Their shadows reached the metal barrier long before they did.

When Kilgore saw that the padlock was fastened, his shoulders sagged. The breath went out of him. His right hand, shaking noticeably, grabbed at his chin, then worked its way up his face and onto his head, dislodging his Bees cap.

"Maybe we're early," he said, though without any hope at all.

As Traveler stooped to recover the cap, he saw the corner of an envelope tucked beneath the door. It started to tear when he pulled on it.

"Be careful, for Christ's sake," Kilgore said, dropping to one knee. "Here, let me do that."

Traveler stood to one side while Kilgore struggled to free the envelope. In the end, it took both of them—Traveler wedging a jack handle under the metal door while Kilgore kept up a gentle pressure on the envelope—to liberate the message.

Kilgore read it once to himself and then out loud to Traveler. "Sorry about standing you up tonight, but Pepper called and told me you weren't to do anything at the park until he's spoken to you personally. There's been a change in plans, he said, and he wants you to get in touch with him immediately. In the meantime, don't do anything. Your fan, Hal."

"Goddammit." Kilgore's face looked dead white in the headlight beams. "There must be some mistake. If something had come up, Pepper would have told me so on the phone."

"I don't understand what's going on here, Hap. Your grounds keeper friend works for the Saints. So why would he be taking orders from Pepper?"

"Maybe the sale has gone through already."

"You don't believe that."

"Christ. I don't know what to think anymore. But Hal's a Bees fan from way back. He wants to see Pepper running things as much as I do."

"Maybe. But he's putting his job on the line in the meantime."

"I've got to talk to Pepper," Kilgore said.

"That makes two of us."

34

ON THE WAY BACK to the Phoebe Clinton Home, Kilgore asked to be dropped off at the mint, a bar on Second South. Instead, Traveler persuaded him to come home with him and have dinner first. But there was no food on the table, only an old Monopoly game that Martin had dug out of the basement.

As soon as the three of them were seated around the Monopoly board—with an old coffee can at Kilgore's elbow to catch tobacco drippings—Martin explained the rules. Namely, that his prospective fatherhood depended on finding Claire, whose whereabouts revolved around the game in front of them.

"This was her last communication," Martin concluded, holding up the Community Chest card.

As one, they leaned over the board to study the Community Chest square on the playing board. It was surrounded by property with yellow markings: St. James Place, Tennessee Avenue and New York Avenue.

Traveler recognized the clue immediately. "Before we moved in together," he said, "Claire had a garage apartment out by the airport. On New York Avenue."

The city map made a liar of him. It was New York Drive, a block-long road between Bloomfield and Mandalay.

"You're both crazy," Kilgore said. "Why would you want to find a woman who's suing you?"

Martin tapped the side of his head. "The question is, why would my son take up with such a woman in the first place?"

Kilgore looked at Traveler as if expecting an answer.

"I'll tell you," Martin went on. "Some women are like a disease that you catch. Only there's no real cure. The symptoms go away from time to time, but they come back the moment you relax your guard. Isn't that so, Moroni?"

The ringing phone kept Traveler from admitting just how close his father was to the truth.

"It's me, Willis," Tanner said. "I'm in Fillmore. And guess what? Pepper Dalton is here, too."

"I don't like the sound of that."

"We're about to take possession of Glory. We've got a court order and intend to serve it at first light in the morning."

"Why are you telling me this?"

"You asked for my help, didn't you?"

"I can tell from the sound of your voice that the church is involved."

Tanner cleared his throat. "I ought to tell you that Pepper's changed. He's not the way I remembered him at all. He's . . . I don't know how to explain it."

"More to the point," Traveler said, "how are you going to get past Zeke Eldredge?"

"The sheriff's rounded up a small army of deputies."

"Is this a straight eviction, Willis, or are you looking to pin a killing on Zeke?"

"We go in at dawn whether you're here or not, Mo."

"Is that an invitation?"

"I do God's work. That's all."

"To get there in time, I'll have to fly in."

"I'll be waiting for you," Tanner said, and hung up.

Traveler went into the kitchen to make a pot of coffee.

"It will keep you up all night," Martin said as soon as he and Kilgore were seated at the kitchen table.

"That's the point. I'm on my way to Glory."

Martin and Kilgore shook their heads at the same time. Martin said, "That's a long way to drive in the dark. And on bad mountain roads."

"I was hoping you'd fly me."

"Who's paying for the airplane?"

Kilgore gestured surrender with his hands. "Don't look at me."

"Willis Tanner is already in Fillmore," Traveler said. "He and Pepper Dalton. They're going to evict Zeke and his flock first thing in the morning."

Martin nodded. "That's something I'd like to see."

"Me, too," Kilgore said, "if you have room for another passenger.

"Why not?" Martin went to phone the airport.

35

WILLIS TANNER HAD A CAR waiting for them at the airstrip just outside Fillmore. The car's headlights, plus those of two other vehicles, were the only landing beacons. Tanner himself was behind the wheel.

As Willis chauffeured them through the night, Traveler tried not to think about the road in front of them. But his memory refused to cooperate. It kept projecting images of the switchbacks, gully crossings and precipices that had to be negotiated before they reached the top of the Pavant Plateau.

No one spoke for a long time. The only sound inside the car was Kilgore's nervous, open-mouthed gum chewing in the backseat. Finally Martin, who was sitting next to Kilgore, said, "Have you ever been to Glory before, Willis?"

"Only when I read my scriptures." Tanner snorted and raised his hands off the wheel as if seeking applause from heaven.

Traveler braced himself in the passenger's seat. "For Christ's sake, be careful."

"There's no need to blaspheme." Tanner's hands fell back onto the wheel and stayed there. "Actually, I visited Glory sometime back, before Zeke Eldredge and his bunch moved in. It's been off-limits to us ever since."

"Who is us?" Kilgore wanted to know.

"By my reckoning," Tanner responded, ignoring the question, "we ought to reach Glory about daylight."

"What about Pepper?" Kilgore persisted. "You told Moroni that he was with you."

"Not exactly with me, only in the same town. By now he and the sheriff are well ahead of us."

Martin said, "Are you sure you know what you're doing, Willis? I don't like the idea of running into a man like Eldredge by mistake in the dark."

"Do you think he's the killer, then?"

"My son's the expert. Ask him."

"Well?" Tanner said.

"Somehow I don't think so," Traveler answered, the words expelled before he'd thought them through consciously. But now that they were out in the open, he realized that he believed them. At the gut level at least, the same locality that was beginning to tell him things he'd rather not hear.

"If we haven't come here to rid ourselves of a man like Eldredge," Kilgore said, "then why the hell have we been traveling all night?"

"To find out what the hell's going on," Traveler said. "Besides, the more I think about it, the more convinced I am that Zeke may be in need of some impartial witnesses."

"Don't count on me for that," Tanner said. "To my way of thinking the man already stands convicted of things worse than murder."

Traveler stared at Tanner, trying to read his expression in the glow of green light coming from the dashboard. "Why am I here, Willis? And why the red-carpet treatment?"

"Like you said, Mo. It's always good to have witnesses."

"You can do better than that."

"All right. You know how the church feels about polygamists and publicity. That's why we want someone like yourself, an independent observer, here to see that everything is done in a lawful manner."

Knowing Tanner, the response was probably filled with half-truths. The problem was to sort them out.

"I'll say a prayer for you," Tanner added.

"Amen," Kilgore said, and leaned forward to clutch the back of the seat. "Remember, Mo. I hired you to protect Pepper, not someone like Zeke Eldredge."

Before Traveler could answer, the car topped a steep rise. A mile or so ahead of them, a spurt of flame vented from the earth. Until that moment, he hadn't realized how far they had come. Traveler licked his lips and tasted the coal smoke that rose continually from the earth around Glory.

36

Sunrise revealed a smoke-filled sky and half a dozen sheriff's units blocking the road to Glory. Willis Tanner parked behind the last vehicle in a line. The entrance to the main mine shaft, where Traveler had gone into the earth with Zeke Eldredge only two days before, lay a hundred yards up the dirt road.

Emmett Culverwell detached himself from a group of three law officers at the head of the line of cars and came to greet them. "I got your message, Mr. Tanner. It's good to see you again. We've been waiting for you to get here."

"And Eldredge?" Tanner asked.

"We've got him cornered."

Dawn light turned Tanner's reaction into a malicious grin. He wiped it away with the back of his hand before asking Culverwell for a full report.

"We tried to sneak in under the cover of darkness," the sheriff began. "But they must have had a sentry posted somewhere. By the time we were in position, the whole bunch of them were holed up in the old shaft building up there. We don't know if they're armed or not."

Sheriff Culverwell, who had been wearing bib overalls the first time Traveler met him, was now in full uniform, which included a gun belt and a .357 magnum. He no longer wore his severe, no-nonsense glasses, though the indentations of their rims remained in the skin around his eyes.

Traveler swallowed. His throat felt gritty from coal dust. "I didn't see any guns when I was here."

"You were one man, so there was no need for firepower on their part."

"Are the women and children in there too?"

The sheriff started back up the road, indicating that Tanner and Traveler were to follow him. Martin and Kilgore stayed put.

"Everyone's inside," the sheriff said, moving slowly to make conversation easier. "Women, kids, cattle and sheep for all I know. They heard us coming and took cover."

"Even so, there's no reason to think they'll start shooting," Traveler said.

"These fundamentalists don't think like we do," Tanner put in.

"That's right," the sheriff said. "They shed your blood and say it's for your own good. That's what they said to you, wasn't it? When they beat the shit out of you, Traveler? Blood atonement for your sins."

"You've got an army here," Traveler said, pointing to the ring of officers, all armed with shotguns, surrounding the mine. As he did so, sunlight touched the building's dilapidated clapboard siding, turning it to gold. The lettering, GLORY MINE 1881, seemed to catch fire.

"The timbers holding up that place were rotten a quarter of a century ago when I used to hike around here as a kid," Sheriff Culverwell said. "God knows what they're like now. The whole place should have been torn down years ago. That's why I've told my deputies to hold their ground and stay put. They're mostly part-timers anyway." He pointed a finger at the pioneer cemetery on the hill. "And I don't feel like delivering bad news to any new widows. That's what I told the district attorney before I left

Fillmore. That I would follow the law, not church commandments, on this one."

When they reached the lead car a civilian got out. Traveler assumed it was the district attorney in question, a balding man wearing an overlarge raincoat that failed to hide his potbelly. Thick-lensed, misty glasses masked his eyes. As he closed the car door, he stumbled in a deep rut and flailed his arms in hopes of catching hold of something to keep his balance. Traveler came to his aid.

Once he'd steadied himself, the man scowled at Traveler, pushing him aside in order to confront Willis Tanner. "You should have been here earlier. They wouldn't listen to me and use their guns. Now it's too late. Or so says our sheriff. But what about you? Will the church overrule him?"

"Who the hell are you?" Traveler said.

"Pepper!" someone shouted.

Traveler turned around to see Hap Kilgore lumbering forward, Martin right behind him.

Kilgore bypassed Traveler to throw his arms around the man in the raincoat. They hugged and pounded each other on the back.

Traveler felt his mouth hanging open. He snapped it shut and shook his head. Then he closed his eyes. But when he opened them a moment later nothing had changed. There was still no sign of the graceful shortstop he'd idolized as a boy. Number 22 on the old Bees, a blue-eyed, blond-haired all-American boy right off the cover of the *Saturday Evening Post*.

Kilgore broke the hug to say, "This is the man I was telling you about. Moroni Traveler. Mo, meet Pepper."

Dalton took off his glasses to shake hands. His eyes were blue as ever. "Sorry. I should have recognized you."

"I know the feeling," Traveler said.

Martin grumbled. "I feel cheated."

The flicker of a smile crossed Dalton's face before he

turned away to concentrate on Tanner. "I was told that you'd have Eldredge taken care of by dawn."

"Wait a minute," Traveler said. "Are we here to evict or arrest?"

Tanner said, "There are charges outstanding against Mr. Eldredge. Bigamy. Trespassing. Each on its own warrants arrest."

"Does Zeke know that?" Traveler said.

Tanner deferred to the sheriff, who said, "We told him on the bullhorn. We read him his rights too."

"That's it, then," Dalton said. "You've done your duty."

Tanner nodded. "He's right, sheriff. It's time we got on with it."

Culverwell shook his head. "The way I see it, the best thing to do is wait out Zeke and his flock."

The ground trembled. Flame vented from a small fissure in the road halfway between the mine entrance and where they stood. Even as they watched, the fissure grew. More flame erupted from it. The road was now impassible.

"That sucker opened up just after we arrived," Culverwell said. "We thought it was an earthquake at first. You should have seen us scatter. For a minute there—"

"Watch it," one of the deputies called out.

The door to the mine was opening slowly. Traveler stepped in front of his father.

"I call on God to open the earth again and swallow you up," Eldredge shouted as his bald head emerged into the morning light.

Culverwell cupped his hands around his mouth. "Come out with your hands up, Zeke. We'll hold our fire."

"The Antichrist is among you."

"You know me, Zeke. Emmett Culverwell."

"You're right. I know a bishop of the damned when I see one."

"You can say whatever you like, Zeke, as long as we don't have any bloodshed."

Blurred faces, little more than smudges actually, appeared behind Eldredge.

"I'll make you an offer," Eldredge bellowed. "We'll settle this once and for all. Me against the Antichrist. A fight to the death. Winner take all." He pointed at the fresh chasm that had split open the road. "We'll meet at the edge of Satan's pit, the newest opening into hell."

"He means me," Dalton said.

Hap Kilgore grabbed Traveler's arm. "We can't let Pepper fight him."

"Relax," the sheriff said. "Nobody's going to fight."

Eldredge shouted, "Either you meet my terms or our blood will be on your hands."

"We don't have to shoot to get you out of there, Zeke," the sheriff called back. "We've got tear gas."

"And we have explosives. We'll set them off if we have to."

"He's right," Traveler said. "I saw boxes of dynamite when I was in there."

"Why the hell didn't you say so before?" Culverwell said.

"It didn't seem important."

Culverwell rubbed the indentations his glasses had left around his eyes. Finally he cupped his hands and called to Eldredge. "Zeke, we need some time to talk this over."

"Sixty seconds," the man replied, and retreated back inside, closing the door behind him.

"Do you think he'll explode the dynamite?" Martin asked nobody in particular.

"Mo," Tanner said, "how many people does he have here in Glory?"

"About fifty. Most of them are women and children."

Tanner shook his head. "We can't have something like that."

"He could be bluffing," the sheriff said.

"It doesn't matter," Dalton responded. "All we have to

do is pretend to agree to his terms. When he comes out into the open you shoot him. And that's the end of it."

"I'm not shooting anybody without provocation," the sheriff said.

Dalton pointed at Willis Tanner. "What about you? What do you say?"

The door opened again. "Time's up," Eldredge cried. "Do I light the fuse or not?"

Tanner took a step toward Dalton and said, "There's no flock without a shepherd."

"That's my point. Shoot him and it's all over."

Tanner shook his head. "It's your fight at the moment."

"You're crazy if you think I'm going up against a man like that."

Hap Kilgore edged closer to Dalton.

"All I'm saying," Tanner said, "is that I can't authorize a shooting. What we have to do is get our hands on Eldredge. Once we have him, the others will surrender quickly enough."

Dalton thumbed himself in the chest. "Don't talk about we when you mean me."

"It's always good to have friends in high places."

"Only if you're alive," Dalton said.

"I'll go up against him with you, Pepper," Kilgore said. "Like the old days. You and me together."

"You heard Eldredge. He wants me, man to man."

Kilgore took a step toward the mine and shouted, "I'm the one you want. I'm the Antichrist."

The door opened again. "Come closer so I can get a better look at you, old man."

"I'll show you who's an old man."

Traveler made a grab to restrain Kilgore but missed.

"Shit," Dalton said, and reluctantly followed Kilgore toward the smoking fissure. Traveler went with him.

As soon as the three of them reached the fissure, Eldredge stepped out into the open. He was wearing the same baggy black suit.

Carefully, never taking his eyes from them, Eldredge stripped off his coat. Then he removed his *Book of Mormon* from one of the pockets before dropping the garment to the ground.

"The devil fears me," he said. "I can see that plain enough. He sends three against one. And yet goodness will triumph in the end."

He held the book aloft. The paper marker still fluttered between its pages.

Out of the corner of his eye, Traveler saw deputies begin moving toward the open doorway, where many of Eldredge's followers had crowded together to watch their shepherd. As for Eldredge, he calmly walked to the other side of the fissure, which was now a good ten feet across, too far to jump from a standing start.

Traveler cast a quick look into the pit. Ten feet below ground level was a crust of glowing coals. The fumes rising from them were sulfuric enough to make him believe the devil himself had stoked the fire.

Eldredge stepped to the brink and peered down. Heat waves rising from the fissure made him shimmer. "It's like an open mouth, isn't it? But whose mouth? If we step inside, who swallows us? God or Satan?"

He lowered *The Book of Mormon* until it was pointing across the chasm at Traveler. "Back off, big man. Otherwise I signal my flock and we're all blown to hell."

Traveler glanced toward the doorway, which was no more than fifty feet away. He saw no sign of dynamite or detonator. The deputies still had a long way to go.

"All it takes is a match," Eldredge said.

Clenching his teeth, Traveler moved back a pace.

"Farther."

He took another step.

"This is no game we're playing," Eldredge snapped. "My soul's at stake. My salvation."

Traveler backed up three paces and then folded his arms to indicate there would be no more compromise.

Eldredge grinned. "Three to one or ten to one. It makes no difference. God is with me."

Slowly he began circling the pit. Both Dalton and Kilgore moved too, keeping pace with him, keeping the flaming chasm between them. They'd completed half a circle, with Eldredge just coming into Traveler's range, when the man changed direction.

When they were back in their original positions, Eldredge stopped and removed the marker from his *Book of Mormon*. "Do you know what this is, Pepper? It's the end of all your plans. The end of your blasphemy."

"What's he talking about?" Kilgore asked.

Pepper only shook his head.

"It's my marriage license to your sister." Eldredge waved the document. "Alive or dead, this gives me half of Glory. Me or my heirs. There's no way you can ever have this land for yourself."

Holding the paper out in front of him, Eldredge began circling the pit again. When Dalton moved off to keep the abyss between them, Hap Kilgore stayed put.

"Talk to me, Pepper," Kilgore implored. "Tell me he's crazy."

Dalton said nothing.

"I'll explain for you, old man," Eldredge said. "This piece of paper means I have only one wife." A sound came from him, half laugher, half scream. All of it played hell with Traveler. "The rest of my women are only mistresses as far as the law is concerned."

Kilgore stared at Dalton. "Is that true?"

Dalton glanced at Traveler before answering. "We won't know until it goes to court."

"How long will that take?" Kilgore asked.

"Years," Eldredge answered. "You know the courts. You'll never see that baseball team of yours."

Kilgore kept his eyes on Dalton. "That message you left at Derks. You said there'd been a change of plans. Is this it?"

"Hap, I promise you. As far as I knew the Bees were ours. That note was part of a surprise. You weren't going to be my third base coach. I was going to name you manager. Just like the old days. Now I guess we're both out of luck.'.'

Kilgore groaned, spitting words and tobacco at Eldredge. "You bastard. You—" He choked.

Traveler sucked air, fueling himself with oxygen and adrenaline, as he edged closer to Kilgore. Eldredge saw him do it but merely smiled and kept coming closer himself.

"I still have my team in Fillmore," Dalton said. "It's not much, Hap, only semipro. But we can make something out of it, the two of us together."

Traveler reached Hap's side and touched him gently for reassurance. But the old man shook him off.

"Stay away from me, Moroni. I mean it."

His outburst brought Eldredge to an abrupt stop five feet away. Five feet from Hap, more from Traveler. Too far to make a move with any certainty of success.

"I did it, Mo," Kilgore said, and took a step toward Eldredge. "I killed them both, Prissy and Kate."

Traveler denied it with a shake of his head. A woman had killed them. Witnesses had said so, though one of the witnesses, Kate, was also a victim.

"I'm sorry about Kate. I didn't want to hurt her. I made sure she was unconscious before I cut her throat." He pointed a finger at Eldredge. "Here I am. The evil one you seek."

Eldredge twitched. His head swung from Kilgore to Dalton and back again.

Traveler made his move, but too late.

Kilgore had already launched himself at Eldredge, catching the man by surprise, carrying him in a bear hug to the edge of the abyss. For an instant they teetered there, Kilgore's back to Traveler while Eldredge's terrified face hung over the old man's shoulder.

As they began to topple backward into the pit, Eldredge reached out with the hand that held the marriage certificate. His fingers opened, either to hand over the document or to grab hold of Traveler and take him with them into the chasm.

Traveler did his best, but all he caught was paper.

Screaming, the two men burst through the crust of glowing coals and disappeared into the earth. Their cries died before the stream had time to sizzle up after them.

In the confusion, nobody saw Traveler pocket the certificate.

37

A SPURT OF FRESH flame, fed by human fuel, erupted from the pit. With it came a spitting sound and the stench of burning flesh. Pepper Dalton turned and bolted toward the sheriff.

But Traveler felt rooted to the earth. Breath caught in his throat. His esophagus spasmed against rising bile. His fists clenched in anger, anger at himself. He should have foreseen Hap's reaction; he should have saved the old man.

Finally it dawned on him that he, too, had to move, had to back away from the mine shaft and its explosive content. But he needn't have bothered, because Willis Tanner had been right. A flock is lost without its shepherd. Eldredge's death had spurred a mass exodus of followers from the building, all blinking against the light of day and the even harsher reality that now faced them.

Their sudden evacuation triggered a response from the deputies, who quickly jacked fresh shells into their shotguns. Women cringed against the deadly sound. Children caught their mothers' fear and began to cry. Their wailing brought life to the bedraggled men, who began looking around in frustration for someone to blame, someone to attack. The deputies, Traveler saw from his position on this side of the abyss, were the targets closest at hand.

"Everyone put your hands up," he shouted, thrusting his own arms into the air by way of example. "And don't move."

"Do as he says," one of the deputies picked up. "That way, no one else gets hurt."

Gradually, the flock complied, with mothers showing the younger children what was expected of them. By the time Sheriff Culverwell joined Traveler, the congregation was being lined up against the mine's clapboard siding.

"For Christ's sake," Culverwell exploded. "Get them away from there. There's dynamite inside."

"I'll go in and check it," Traveler said. "I know where to look."

The boxes labeled DYNAMITE, originally stored far underground in the tunnel, were now stacked head high just inside the door. But there was no sign of a fuse or detonator, or even a trail of powder.

He reported that fact to the sheriff, who still insisted on clearing the immediate area, directing his deputies to assemble the Flock of Zion at the foot of Cemetery Hill. As soon as they were well on their way, Dalton and Willis Tanner joined Traveler and the sheriff, who were once again staring down into the fissure. Martin had opted to rest in one of the police vehicles.

"I suppose there's no sense in probing for the bodies," the sheriff observed. "Not until the area burns itself out. By then, of course, there won't be anything left but ashes."

"God's own cremation," Dalton said.

"Or the devil's," Tanner responded, as if speaking for Eldredge.

Dalton pounced on the comment. "That's right. Traveler heard Hap confess. He heard him say he was the evil one."

"I heard him," Traveler agreed. "But I'm not sure I believe it. I think he was protecting you."

Dalton held out his arms. "My hands are clean in this. Everybody saw what happened."

"With his dream of rejoining the Bees dead, Hap had nothing left," Tanner said.

"You're forgetting Mary Cook," Traveler said. "I saw them together. Hap had a lot to live for."

"That's your interpretation," Dalton said. "But he was an old man living in the past."

"And yet you were going to name him your new manager?"

Dalton's lips curled away from his teeth. "Are you joking? An old fool like that? Never."

"Third base coach then?"

"I've already been through this with Hap's so-called girlfriend, that old dame at the nursing home. He was going out to pasture, no doubt about it."

"And that's what the note at Derks Field was all about?"

"Hold it," the sheriff interrupted, gesturing for silence. "You two can talk baseball later. Right now I want to know what was said out here before Kilgore and Eldredge took the fall."

Nodding eagerly, Dalton recounted Hap's confession. When Traveler's turn came, he confirmed Hap's words but not their meaning.

"There's something else to consider," Traveler added. "Kate Ferguson's neighbor saw only one visitor on the day of the murder, a woman."

"I spoke with that neighbor too," the sheriff said. "It was getting dark at the time, so she could have been mistaken."

"And what about Priscilla's killing?" Traveler persisted. "Kate Ferguson told me she was in the hotel that day. She saw a woman there, too. In broad daylight. She thought she could identify her if she ever saw her again."

"I'll let the Salt Lake police worry about that. As far as I'm concerned, I've got a valid confession to the murder of Kate Ferguson."

"Don't forget the tobacco at the scene of the crime," Dalton added. "That backs up Hap's story. He chewed just like Zeke did."

Traveler shook his head. "Look around you. Half the women here chew tobacco."

Sheriff Culverwell looked to Willis Tanner. "What do you make of this?"

"Speaking for myself, I see no reason to complicate matters unnecessarily."

Traveler knew only too well that his friend seldom spoke for himself.

"What about the document Eldredge claimed to have?" Traveler said. "His one and only marriage license. The one that proved him monogamous."

"Nobody believes a man like Zeke Eldredge," Dalton said.

"There ought to be a record of that license somewhere," Traveler responded.

"Whatever it was," Tanner said, "it's gone now. I think it best to leave it that way."

Meaning any additional records could be counted on to disappear, should the church so choose.

"Who are you speaking for now, Willis?" Traveler asked, reaching into his pocket to reassure himself that he still had the document.

"You're forgetting something, Mo. Deseret Coal, which is buying Glory from Dalton, belongs to us now."

Now was not the time to use the document, Traveler decided. Not out here where he was outnumbered. His hand came out of his pocket empty. "I seem to remember you telling me that the church wasn't involved."

Tanner bowed his head. "I think it's time we all prayed for the dead."

38

By LATE AFTERNOON Traveler and his father were back at the Salt Lake Airport. The weather had turned sullen once again, as had Willis Tanner, who'd hitched a ride in their plane. As head of public relations for the church, he warned them to keep their mouths shut until an official press release could be issued from the Hotel Utah. Then he retrieved his car from the executive parking area, leaving them to walk half a mile to where they'd left the Jeep.

Rain-soaked and suffering from lack of sleep, father and son drove to the Chester Building.

"I know you need rest," Traveler said as they left the car in the loading zone. "I'll take you home after I check the answering machine."

"Don't worry about me. I understand how you feel about Hap. You do what you have to."

For once the lobby was empty. Even Nephi Bates had abandoned his post. His portable cassette player was hanging from the starter's handle. Out of it poured hymns from the Tabernacle Choir.

Traveler ran the elevator himself. When they reached the third floor, he smelled the pot smoke before he saw it. It was seeping beneath their office door.

Inside, Mad Bill and Charlie Redwine were reclining in the clients' chairs, their bare feet gripping the lip of Traveler's desk. An empty jug of Martin's red wine stood nearby.

"Barney let us in out of the rain," Bill said as soon as he saw the look on Martin's face. "He didn't know when you were going to be back, and we didn't have any place else to go."

"We were wet," Charlie added.

The smell coming from Bill's ankle-length robe was a cross between mildewed carpet nap and wet dog fur.

"We've earned our keep," Bill said, his big toe moving across the desk top to nudge a notepad. "We've been taking messages just like secretaries."

"Who called?" Traveler asked.

Bill retracted his feet and stood up. "Home Run Cecil, he called himself. If you ask me, he was drunk."

"Anyone else?"

Bill pointed at the window to indicate the temple beyond.

"Do you mean Willis Tanner?" Traveler asked.

"Who else?"

Sighing, Martin eased behind his desk and sat down. He spun his chair until he was pointing toward the Hotel Utah, which was directly across the street from the temple. "I'd give a lot to be a fly on the wall in the prophet's penthouse."

Traveler picked up the phone. His father lifted his extension to listen in.

When Traveler got through to the Stratford Hotel in Baltimore, he was tempted to ask for Home Run Cecil. But that had been the man's nickname in the old Pioneer League. In the big leagues, he'd had to settle for plain Chuck.

"Mr. Cecil, this is Moroni Traveler in Salt Lake City. I'm a friend of Hap Kilgore's."

"Goddamn. Salt Lake brings back memories, let me tell you. I had a hell of a year in that town of yours. I hit three-twenty-eight with thirty-one homers. Hap's cleanup hitter, that was me. How the hell is the old boy anyway? He's getting along in years, but then aren't we all."

"I'm a private detective, Mr. Cecil. Hap hired me to look into a problem for him."

"If Hap's in trouble, I'm your man. Call me Chuck, by the way."

"Did you know that Pepper Dalton is about to buy the baseball team here in Salt Lake?"

"I'll be goddamned. He always said he would. But I figured it was just bullshit."

"He's going to name them the Bees again."

"Let me tell you something, Moroni. I trade and sell baseball cards for a living. Some say, my wife included, that it's not fit work for a grown man. But I do okay. Good enough, in fact, to tell you right now, I'll be there sitting in the box seats on the first base line when they throw out the first ball. You can tell Hap I'll pay for his seat too, and a dinner on the town to boot."

"Pepper's been talking about naming Hap his new manager."

"By God, he must have changed, because that doesn't sound like the Pepper Dalton I remember. A bunch of us used to sit around the clubhouse and talk about what we wanted to do with our lives. Me, I wanted the big leagues. I made it, too. For a year. But Pepper couldn't hit. So he wanted a team of his own. 'When I get one,' he used to say, 'I'm going to manage it myself.'"

"What else can you tell me about him?" Traveler asked.

"I always thought not being able to hit did something to him. You know, soured him. He never laughed unless the laugh was on somebody else. And he was a trouble-maker."

"How do you mean?"

"It's been a long time, you've got to understand that. Offhand I don't remember anything specific. But he liked to spread rumors. That I do recall. Rumors about trades, big league scouts being in the stands, things like that. He got a kick out of stirring up the other players. To my way of thinking, it was his way of getting back at those of us who could hit.

"Thinking back on it, Pepper was what you'd call an operator. Manipulating people, that was his specialty. One of his rumors, I remember now, got a couple of guys so nervous they went into slumps. But maybe that's what it takes to be a good manager. I don't know. Me, I'll vote for the Hap Kilgores of this world. There, by God, is a man with a real sense of humor."

Cecil's laughter was so loud it created static. "Let me tell you what he used to do. He had this woman's wig he'd put on that bald head of his. The first time he did it, he wore a dress too and walked right into our shower room. You should have seen the guys run for cover. But then that red-faced complexion of his made him one hell of a convincing-looking woman."

Martin snapped his fingers for attention and mouthed, "It's true, then. Hap must have killed them."

Traveler, suffering a flash of better-late-than-never enlightenment, shook his head and held up one finger.

"If Hap tried that these days," Cecil continued, "they'd call him a pervert."

39

TRAVELER DROPPED HIS FATHER off at the house and changed his clothes before driving on to the Phoebe Clinton Home. By the time he parked under the porte cochere, the eastern half of the valley, including the home, was in bright sunlight. Cloud covered the west side of town.

Traveler turned his back on the cold wind blowing off the lake and rang the bell. Golly Simpson answered, wearing a white uniform and a forced smile. His head started shaking before Traveler could open his mouth.

"Sorry," Simpson said through a grim smile. "Visiting hours have been cut short today. In fact, we're no longer accepting residents, since the home will be closing soon. Permanently as far as we know."

"I'd like to see your sister," Traveler said.

"Were you the one who called her about Hap?"

Traveler shook his head. "That was the sheriff in Fillmore."

"Mary's ill. She has been ever since the call. The fact is, she should be in a hospital if I'm any judge."

"I can't leave without seeing her," Traveler said, crossing the threshold and forcing Simpson to retreat.

"Sure, a big man like you enjoys shoving little people around."

Traveler started down the hall leading to the solarium where he'd talked to Mary once before.

"She's in her room," Simpson said. "She told me you'd be coming here sooner or later and that you should be shown in to see her when you did. If it were up to me, I'd call the police."

Mary's room was on the second floor front. Her brother knocked and opened the door in one motion. "Mr. Traveler is here," he announced gently before stepping to one side to allow Traveler to enter by himself. "I'll be right out here in the hall if you need me, Mary."

Soft light came from a small shaded lamp on the nightstand next to the narrow hospital-style bed where the woman lay. Heavy velvet drapes, the same deep blue as the worn carpet, were drawn across the two west-facing windows. Judging by the size of the room, it had been designed as a master suite when the mansion was first built.

Mary pressed a button on the small control unit she was holding. A motor whirred and the head of the bed began to rise. She didn't stop it until she was sitting up.

"I've been waiting for you," she said. "Please, come sit by me."

A straight-backed metal chair was already positioned beside the bed. As soon as he was seated near her, Traveler saw just how much she'd changed. Her face, round and fleshy only yesterday, now looked tight and drawn. Her skin had taken on that translucent quality that comes after a long illness. Her eyes, red-rimmed and swollen, looked too large for her head.

"I've been lying here waiting for you ever since I heard about Hap," she said.

"I'm sorry."

"I know that."

He took a deep breath. The room smelled vaguely medicinal. "Why don't you save us both a lot of time and trouble and tell me what really happened?"

The tendons in her neck pulled tight as she raised her head away from the pillows stacked behind her back. "We have dreams, Mr. Traveler. That's the trouble. We dream things that aren't to be." She sighed. Her head sagged back.

When he reached out to comfort her she drew away from him. "Thank you just the same, but we both know that won't do any good."

"I could come back later, when you're feeling better."

She dismissed that suggestion with a wave of her hand. "We were doomed when Pepper Dalton came to us. With that smile of his, that charm, he told us about Glory and about his sister's involvement with that man, Zeke Eldredge. He said it was Zeke's influence that made his Priscilla turn against her own brother. Made her refuse to sell Glory. He asked us to help change her mind."

"Why would he come to you?"

Mary's head moved in jerks and starts as she looked around the room. "Because that way, Pepper said, we could all realize our dreams. Hap could return to his old Bees. I would be able to save my nursing home. 'We'll share and share alike,' he said. 'There will be money enough for everybody.'"

She paused to wipe the tears from her eyes. "He said he'd finally convinced Priscilla to come to Salt Lake and talk things over. 'She's coming around. I know it,' he kept saying. 'All we've got to do now is nail her down.' That was our job, me and Hap, to convince her that we deserved her trust. That we'd use our share of the money to help the elderly here at the home. 'Make her love you,' Pepper kept saying. 'I know Prissy. You do that and she'll be a push-over.'"

"And was she?"

"We did our best. We went to see her at the Semloh Hotel just like Pepper asked. Do you know what she did when we told her our plans? Laughed in our face, that's what. She said it was her joke on Pepper, because she'd come to Salt Lake only pretending to waver, to taunt him."

"How did Pepper react to that?"

"That wasn't all Prissy had to say. She told us she was going to see an attorney while she was here in town. Once that was done, she said, her brother would never get his hands on Glory."

Traveler touched the document that he'd transferred to his shirt pocket when he changed clothes. "Did she say why?"

"She laughed about it. She said she'd found the one way to keep a polygamist faithful. When I asked her what that meant, she said it was none of my business. In fact, that's when she asked Hap and me to leave."

"But you came back."

"The sheriff told me that Hap confessed to both murders. That you were a witness to what he said."

"I heard what he said, all right. But I didn't believe all of it. You know that. Otherwise I wouldn't be here."

Her head twitched, a single nod. "Hap said you were smart, that he shouldn't have hired you."

"Why did he, then?"

"He didn't realize it was me he was protecting at first. He thought it was Pepper."

"I spoke with one of the old Bees. He told me about Hap and his woman's wig. It was then I knew he might have been able to get away with a masquerade like that at dusk but never in a hotel in broad daylight."

"Tell me, Mr. Traveler. Do you think they have a use for qualified nurses in prison?"

"I'm certain you'll be needed there."

She was staring straight at him, though her eyes appeared to be focused somewhere else in time. One corner of her mouth twitched as she tried to smile.

"I thought I could change Priscilla's mind, one woman to another, so I went back to her room. That's when Kate Ferguson got a good look at me. I was wearing my nurse's uniform at the time, so there was always the chance that I'd be mistaken for one of the maids. But when I finally told Hap what I'd done, he said we couldn't risk it."

"So his confession was half true. He killed Kate to protect you."

"Neither one of us meant to kill anybody. You've got to understand that. When I went back, Prissy told me why she was doing it. I didn't believe her at the time. I thought she was only being vindictive. I should have known better."

"About what?"

"That her brother is a user of people. That he took us in, me and Hap, just like he does everybody. I should have listened to her. She said Pepper had ruined her life and that now she was going to ruin his in return. 'We women have to stick together,' she said, 'against men like him.' Then she laughed so hard she got hiccups and couldn't talk for a while. I should have walked out then, but I didn't. I got her a glass of water and waited for her to calm down. 'Go back and tell Pepper I'm on his side,' she told me. 'Tell him we'll sell Glory and get rich. Then when the papers are ready to sign I'll laugh in his face.' That's when she started laughing again and showed me a bottle of champagne that Pepper had sent over by messenger in anticipation of a celebration."

Mary's right hand, the one nearest Traveler, raised from the bed. She brought her fingers up close to her face and studied them.

"He'd sent her a ceremonial ball and bat, too, that were to be used on opening day when the new Salt Lake City Bees were his. She was laughing again, trying to open the bottle, when I picked up that bat and hit her. I didn't want to kill her. I wasn't even aiming for her head. It just happened. But when I saw her lying there, I wasn't sorry. All I could think about was Hap getting back into baseball. Maybe I intended to kill her all along for Hap's sake. I don't know. But Pepper's the one I should have killed. He never intended to keep his promises to us."

"I wish we could prove that," Traveler said, and stood up. "You're going to need a lawyer. In this town, Sam Howe has the most juice."

Mary shook her head and closed her eyes. The sigh that escaped her made Traveler wince. He left the room and went looking for Golly Simpson, who'd abandoned his post in the hallway and taken shelter in his sister's office.

"I need some more answers," Traveler told him.

From behind the safety of Mary's desk Simpson said, "You'd better leave. I called the police. They're on their way."

"That's fine. Your sister has something to tell them."

Simpson twitched and started to push back from the desk. Traveler stepped around it, cutting off the man's only route of escape.

"As you said before," Traveler reminded him, "guys like me love shoving people around. So just give me an excuse."

"What do you want to know?"

"Why were you following me that first day at Derks Field?"

"It was Hap I was following."

"Why?"

"Pepper came to me with a proposition. He said he was coming into money and could soon offer me a full-time job. In the meantime, he wanted to know what my future brother-in-law was up to."

"The owner of the Saints, Jessie Gilchrist, told me you were working for him."

"Not really. All he wanted was a buyer. That made him Pepper's man too."

"Like we all were," Traveler said.

40

TRAVELER STOPPED AT THE Brigham Street Pharmacy and had one of their double-thick malts. Its slick consistency, that of motor oil, reminded him of Willis Tanner. The reminiscence sent Traveler to the old-fashioned phone booth in the back.

The church's all-purpose telephone number got him through to an operator who, as Willis liked to say, could get in touch with him day or night. As usual, there was a lag time in running Willis to earth. Traveler waited with LDS Musak: the Mormon Tabernacle Choir's version of the *Hallelujah Chorus*.

When Tanner came on the line he said, "Do you know where I am?"

"Do you want me to guess?"

"No."

"There's something I have to know, Willis."

"Make it quick."

"Why does the church want the Glory mine?"

"You called me here to ask that?"

"Something's come up."

"Mo, I . . . wait a minute. I don't trust you when you sound like that. Has something come unstuck?"

Traveler coughed to give himself time to think over his reply. "They don't make glue like they used to, Willis."

"No you don't, Mo. You won't get me this time. The deal's done. There's no going back."

"If that's the case, it's perfectly safe to tell me all about it."

"You said you had a question."

"You first, Willis. Maybe you'll answer it for me, and that will be the end of it."

"I've talked to the district attorney. He's satisfied that Hap committed both murders. The case is closed."

"Without a formal investigation?"

"That's right. That leaves Pepper Dalton in the clear. He's got an apology for being locked up and has agreed not to sue for false arrest. And we've got our deal with him, signed and sealed. Glory and its mine belong to us now."

"Why?"

"It's our investment in the future. The prophet himself believes a day will come when our survival will depend on having independent resources. There's enough coal in Glory to see the faithful through many a winter. It will be used to secure the faith when Gentile civilization has come to an end. Look to *The Book of Mormon*, my friend. Two Nephi. 'Wherefore, he that fighteth against Zion, both Jew and Gentile, both bond and free, both male and female, shall perish; for they are they who are the whore of all the earth, for they who are not for me are against me, saith our God.' You'll be interested to know that strip-mining starts next month, but only enough to put out the fires."

"Are you saying it was Elton Woolley's idea?"

"God speaks through our prophet. That was one of the first things they taught you in Primary. In any case, I told you early on that he was interested in Glory."

"I don't think you did, Willis."

"Well, I meant to. When you asked me about Deseret Coal and Gas I started looking into the situation. But when I reported it to the prophet, he knew everything in advance. He always does."

"How much money did Dalton get?"

"That's not for me to say. But when the check clears there will be more than enough to buy his baseball team, if that's what you're asking. By the way, a special game has been arranged tomorrow, weather permitting. We're all invited to be there to see him throw out the first ball. Your tickets will be at the will-call window."

"Correct me if I'm wrong, but the prophet doesn't like to lose, does he?"

"I don't like the sound of that."

"I've got Zeke Eldredge's marriage certificate in my pocket."

"It's a forgery."

"How can you be so sure?"

"It doesn't prove a thing."

"You could be right. But once a document like that gets into court, who knows what can happen? Appeals, that kind of thing. Do you really want to take a chance?"

"I hear you now. You have something in mind. You're giving us a way out, is that right?"

"I want justice," Traveler said, and went on to explain Pepper Dalton's role as provocateur in the killings.

"Talk about losing battles in court. You'll never be able to prove anything like that against him."

"That's why I've come to you."

"So what do you want from me, Mo, a miracle?"

"Now that you ask, Willis, that's exactly what I have in mind."

41

THE WEATHER BEGAN CLEARING, perhaps in anticipation of tomorrow's big game, as Traveler drove home. He was thinking of a hot bath and a drink when he stepped through the door and into Claire's arms. She immediately snuggled her head against his chest and locked her hands behind his back.

"Women are fickle," Martin said from the comfort of his favorite reclining chair. Lipstick smudged his lips and one cheek.

Balancing on Traveler's shoes, Claire loosened her hold enough to go on tiptoe to kiss him. She tasted of beer and tobacco and the muskiness of sex.

Gently but resolutely, he broke out of her grasp. She seemed unchanged, her pregnancy hidden beneath a loose flowing smock.

"I waited for you at my old place out on New York Drive," she said.

"Some clues should never be followed up."

"I know you love me," she said, following him to the fireplace where he leaned against the mantel. "There's no use trying to hide it."

"You said the same thing to me before he got here," Martin complained.

"My baby needs a father," she answered.

"May I remind you that I'm the one you're suing," Martin said. "A paternity suit makes a man my age feel young again."

Traveler stared at his father. "Dad, I need a drink."

"Are you trying to get me out of the room?" Martin asked.

"He wants to be alone with me, Dad," Claire said.

"Jesus Christ." Martin kicked his chair into a sitting position and stood up. "I know when I'm not wanted."

Claire moved over to give him a hug. "You can bring me another beer, Dad."

"Too much alcohol isn't good for expectant mothers."

Traveler stepped to Claire's side and eased her onto the vacated recliner. "Dad and I will get you something. You just stay here and rest."

She smiled and leaned back against the cushion. "That's what I like, men waiting on me."

As soon as they were in the kitchen Martin filled two shot glasses with whisky. "To Moroni Traveler the third," he said, raising his glass.

Traveler swallowed the whisky in one gulp. "I just made a deal with Willis. I had to back him into a corner to do it, so there's always the chance he could turn dangerous."

Martin sipped his drink. "Tell me about it."

Traveler had gotten as far as the next day's baseball game when Claire joined them.

"You're taking too long in here," she complained.

"We're having a bachelor party," Martin said, refilling the shot glasses.

"Whose?" She peered from one to the other.

Martin winked at his son. "Tell the truth, Moroni, are you the father of this woman's child?"

"You know the old saying. Like father like son."

"You read my mind," Martin said. "Like I've told you so many times, it doesn't matter who the father is. Genes don't count. The only things that do are love and upbringing."

"I know that," Traveler said. "I've known it ever since I was a kid."

"Well, I don't," Claire said, jamming her hands against her hips.

"He said we're both the father," Traveler translated.

"I can't marry the two of you."

"Who said anything about marriage?" Martin added. "We've decided to adopt the child and raise him ourselves. So you're off the hook. We'll even pay your medical bills."

She grasped her stomach. "You don't expect me to go through this for nothing, do you? You'll have to pay for the child too."

"How much?" Martin asked.

"I haven't decided yet."

"We'll do our best," Traveler said. "You know that."

Claire smiled, either with triumph or derision. Traveler couldn't tell which.

42

THE PEAKS OF THE WASATCH caught fire from the setting sun. Their glow reminded Traveler of Glory and its blazing fissures. The memory steeped his resolution, causing him to smile around clenched teeth just as a recorded bugle call, loud enough to make him wince, thundered over the loudspeakers at Derks Field. The scattered crowd responded with a ragged cheer. In the outfield, pigeons, dislodged from their perches by the coming ball game, strutted gallantly.

"Ladies and gentlemen . . ." the stadium announcer said, pausing until the crowd quieted, ". . . we have a special pregame ceremony tonight. It's my great pleasure to introduce and ask you to welcome Mr. Pepper Dalton."

All the banks of stadium lights came on at once, turning the cloudless sky from blue to black.

Pepper, wearing a uniform top tucked into the waist of his street pants, climbed out of the dugout and waved at the crowd before lumbering toward home plate.

He drew token applause.

A brief, bugled fanfare set up the announcer. "Pepper played shortstop in the old Pioneer League, folks, back in the days when our Saints were known as the Bees. He's back with us tonight, along with some guests, to make a special announcement."

The guests in question, Traveler and Willis Tanner, were occupying box seats directly behind home plate. The seating arrangement had been at Traveler's suggestion and Tanner's insistence.

"But then he'll tell you about that himself right after he honors us by throwing out the first ball."

On cue, the Saints catcher came out of the dugout and trotted to home plate, where he shook hands with Pepper. A photographer emerged from the visitors' dugout to snap their picture. Once that was accomplished, Pepper jogged out to the pitcher's mound, holding on to his stomach to keep it from bouncing. By the time the once-lean shortstop stepped onto the pitching rubber, his chest was heaving. Meager strands of gray hair had come unstuck from his scalp and were hanging limply over his eyes.

The catcher went into his squat. Pepper took a deep breath and threw the ball. It bounced twice before the catcher could trap it.

While Pepper walked back to home plate, Traveler nudged Willis Tanner.

"Everything's taken care of," Tanner responded. "Do you have the document with you?"

"We've already gone through that. You get it when our deal is done."

Tanner sighed. "You can't blame me for trying."

Traveler smiled and leaned back in the uncomfortable metal chair. As a boy sitting in the grandstand with his father he'd always coveted such box seats. He was sorry now that his father wasn't with him to see what high prices did for you. But Martin had decided that his presence might be one witness too many for what Traveler had in mind.

The Saints' batboy strung a hand-held microphone out to home plate and handed it to Pepper. Pepper blew into it once to see that it was working.

"Even as I speak to you, ladies and gentlemen," he began, still breathing heavily, "final papers are being signed in the clubhouse. The Saints will soon belong to me. And as their new owner my first official act is to rename them the Bees."

The crowded responded with a mixture of applause and catcalls.

Pepper waited them out before adding, "I intend to give Salt Lake a winning team."

Traveler whistled and stamped his feet, crunching peanut shells underfoot.

"Now let's play ball," Pepper said.

"Take Me Out to the Ball Game" boomed over the loudspeakers. The crowd sang along halfheartedly.

The Saints, as home team, ran onto the field. Pepper waved to the players before disappearing into the dugout. A couple of minutes later he was back in the box, sitting between Traveler and Willis Tanner.

"God damn." Pepper clenched his fists and gleefully pounded both knees. "You don't know how long I've waited for this moment."

Traveler licked his lips, tasting the residue from an earlier hot dog. "I've been meaning to talk to you about the time you spent in jail. I tried to get in to see you, did you know that?"

"Hap told me."

"If I had, things might have been different."

"Could be," Dalton said. "But what would I have told you, anyway?"

That you were obsessed, Traveler answered to himself. That Hap wanted to be a coach so badly he was willing to kill for it. For you.

Out loud Traveler said, "I might have been able to save your fiancée, for one thing."

Pepper shook his head. "It won't do any good to blame ourselves now."

"It's you I'm blaming."

"Hap told me about you. That's when I decided to tell my jailers about my chest pains. Terrible they were too. The jailers didn't have any choice. They sent me to the hospital, where nobody could talk to me."

His smile made Traveler sit on his hands. It was either that or violence.

Pepper threw back his head and showed his teeth, like a man laughing. But only words came out. "The doctor said it was either indigestion or psychosomatic. What do you think?"

On the field the Saints pitcher hit the first batter for Great Falls. Traveler waited until the man reached first base before asking, "Why is it so important to you to bring back the Bees?"

"Because that was the best time of my life. Can you understand that? Can you understand what it's like to be a professional ballplayer?"

Traveler could, but kept quiet about it.

"It's like nothing else I've ever experienced. My God. Imagine getting paid for doing something you love, that you'd do for nothing. Oh, I know I had trouble hitting. But

I would have gotten better. I knew that, and Hap did too. But the goddamned front office wouldn't listen. 'I'm the best fucking shortstop you've got in the farm system,' I told them on that day they let me go. 'You don't throw a Hall of Fame glove away like that,' I told them. But all they said was, 'No hit, no play.' That's when I told them I'd be back someday and make them eat those words."

"Those people are long gone. Hap included."

"You're missing the point. I'm a man who knows how to win. Otherwise I wouldn't be here."

"You're here because Hap isn't."

Pepper snorted. "He's better off not knowing the truth. That you can't win in this game with old men."

"Have you looked at yourself in the mirror lately?"

"So I'm no kid anymore." He tapped the side of his head. "But I've got it up here. All I need is a couple of young coaches to do my legwork."

"You destroyed Hap on purpose," Traveler said. "Mary Cook too."

"Prove it." He turned so that his back was to Willis Tanner. His voice dropped. "That's why I'm going to be such a great manager. Because I know how to manipulate people. How to make them love me. How to get them to do exactly what I want."

Now was the moment, Traveler thought, struggling to keep his emotions from showing. "Is the money that important to you? That you'd destroy people to get it?"

"I don't give a good goddamn about money. It's only a means to get what I want."

The crack of a bat distracted him. The number-two batter for Great Falls flied out to right field.

"Where was I?" Pepper asked, going on before Traveler had time to tell him. "There's only one thing I've ever really wanted in my life—and that's this baseball team."

"You could always buy something else," Traveler said.

"You still don't understand. It has to be *this* team. Or nothing."

"That's exactly what I was hoping to hear."

Pepper's eyes narrowed. "Don't try playing games with me, Traveler. I'm out of your league."

The next batter hit a routine grounder, a sure double-play ball, to the Saints shortstop. The man bobbled it momentarily and was forced to settle for the out at second base.

"He's no Pepper Dalton, that's for sure," Traveler said.

"I'll work with him. He'll get better."

Traveler smiled. "I don't think so."

Pepper started to get out of his seat but Traveler restrained him. "You can't leave yet. Willis Tanner has something to say to you."

"Goddamn you," Pepper said, but turned toward Tanner just the same. "What is it?"

Applause, triggered by the third out of the inning, overrode Tanner's reply. Tanner repeated himself in a loud voice. "You're not a member of the church, are you?"

Pepper's eyes widened. "I can join. The fact is, I was planning to do just that."

"We Saints never take the Lord's name in vain," Tanner said.

"I'm sorry. I apologize."

"Did you know that it was Brigham Young who first started calling the faithful Saints?"

Pepper swallowed nervously.

"We still do for that matter," Tanner said. "So you can understand why we're protective of the name."

Pepper's head twitched.

"If there are to be Saints in this valley," Tanner went on, "they must belong to us."

Air wheezed through Pepper's nostrils. His mouth snapped open to suck in more oxygen.

"That's why we purchased the ball team."

He gasped. "But I have a commitment. A sale."

Traveler pounded Pepper on the back. "You ought to know better than that. In this valley, the church gets what it wants."

The Saints leadoff hitter stepped to the plate. The accompanying bugle call charge almost drowned out Pepper's anguished cry.

The sound drove Traveler out of the box seats and up the grandstand stairs toward the broadcast booth. Halfway there, he thought he heard the radio announcer calling the game. "That ball's really hit. It's going . . . going . . . it's gone to glory."